Henry W. Longfellow, Horace Elisha Scudder

Evangeline

A tale of Acadie

Henry W. Longfellow, Horace Elisha Scudder

Evangeline
A tale of Acadie

ISBN/EAN: 9783337174651

Printed in Europe, USA, Canada, Australia, Japan

Cover: Foto ©Andreas Hilbeck / pixelio.de

More available books at **www.hansebooks.com**

sued Weekly / Number 1 March 17, 1886

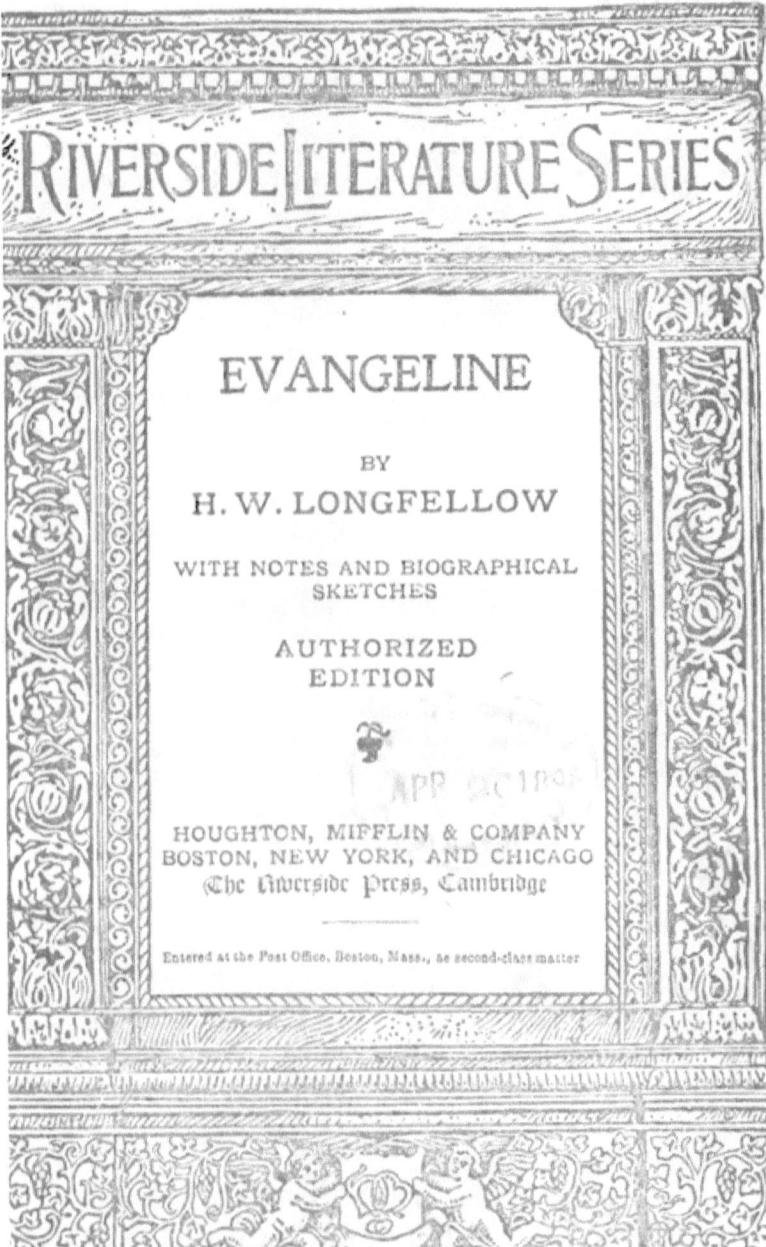

RIVERSIDE LITERATURE SERIES

EVANGELINE

BY

H. W. LONGFELLOW

WITH NOTES AND BIOGRAPHICAL
SKETCHES

AUTHORIZED
EDITION

HOUGHTON, MIFFLIN & COMPANY
BOSTON, NEW YORK, AND CHICAGO
The Riverside Press, Cambridge

Entered at the Post Office, Boston, Mass., as second-class matter

Single Numbers FIFTEEN CENTS   Triple Numbers FORTY-FIVE CENTS
Double Numbers THIRTY CENTS   Quadruple Numbers FIFTY CENTS
Yearly Subscription $5.00

Henry W. Longfellow

The Riverside Literature Series

EVANGELINE

A TALE OF ACADIE

BY

HENRY WADSWORTH LONGFELLOW

*WITH A BIOGRAPHICAL SKETCH,
INTRODUCTION AND NOTES*
BY

H. E. SCUDDER

AND A SKETCH OF LONGFELLOW'S HOME LIFE

BY HIS DAUGHTER

ALICE M. LONGFELLOW

HOUGHTON, MIFFLIN AND COMPANY
Boston : 4 Park Street ; New York : 11 East Seventeenth Street
Chicago : 158 Adams Street
The Riverside Press, Cambridge

The Riverside Press, Cambridge, Mass., U. S. A.
Electrotyped and Printed by H. O. Houghton and Company.

A SKETCH OF THE LIFE AND WRITINGS

OF

HENRY WADSWORTH LONGFELLOW.

I.

THE house is still standing in Portland, Maine, — a large, square, wooden house at the corner of Fore and Hancock streets, — where Longfellow was born, February 27, 1807. Longfellow's early life, however, was passed in what is known as the Longfellow House, a substantial brick mansion in Congress Street. Here lived his father, Stephen Longfellow, and his mother. Zilpha (Wadsworth) Longfellow. The father was a lawyer, who gathered honors through a long life, having been several times a member of the Massachusetts Legislature while Maine was a district of that State; a member of the Hartford Convention, for he was a stout Federalist; a presidential elector when Monroe was first elected; and a member of the United States House of Representatives from 1823 to 1825. He died in 1849, after *Evangeline* had set its seal upon his son's growing reputation. The mother was daughter of General Peleg Wadsworth, who had fought in the Revolutionary War. Both parents were descended from Englishmen, who came to this country in the early days of the colony, and whose successors were marked men in the generations that followed. Upon his mother's side the poet traced his ancestry to four of the Pilgrims who came in the Mayflower, two of these being Elder William Brewster and Captain John Alden.

Henry Wadsworth Longfellow was the second son of the family, which contained four sons and four daughters. He took his name from his mother's brother, Lieutenant Henry Wadsworth, whose heroic death was a fresh and tender memory in the family. Two years and a half before, on the night of September 4, 1804, he had been second in command of the bomb-ketch Intrepid, which was fitted up as an "infernal," and sent stealthily into the harbor of Tripoli to blow up the enemy's fleet. The officers and crew were to apply the match and escape in the boats; but when the Intrepid was still a quarter of a mile from her destination, the watching men in the American fleet outside saw a sudden line of light; in a moment a column of fire shot up from the vessel, and with a tremendous explosion bombs burst in every direction, and the masts and rigging flew into the air. Every soul on board perished. Something, perhaps, of this adventure entered into the poet's early associations, and deepened the ardor of his patriotism.

The sea, at any rate, and a sea-fight nearer home, made a part of his boyish recollections. In 1813, when he was six years old, the American brig Enterprise fell in with the English brig Boxer, outside of Portland harbor, and a fight took place, which could be heard from the shore. It lasted for three quarters of an hour, the Boxer's colors being nailed to the mast. The Enterprise came into the harbor, bringing her captive, but both commanders had been killed in the engagement, and were buried side by side in the cemetery on Mountjoy. In his poem *My Lost Youth*, Longfellow recalls the town as it then was, and this memorable fight: —

> " I remember the black wharves and the ships.
>   And the sea-tides tossing free ;
> And Spanish sailors with bearded lips,
> And the beauty and mystery of the ships,
>   And the magic of the sea.
>   And the voice of that wayward song

MR. LONGFELLOW'S BIRTHPLACE, PORTLAND

Is singing and saying still :
'A boy's will is the wind's will,
And the thoughts of youth are long, long thoughts.'

" I remember the bulwarks by the shore,
  And the fort upon the hill ;
The sunrise gun, with its hollow roar,
The drum-beat repeated o'er and o'er,
  And the bugle wild and shrill.
    And the music of that old song
    Throbs in my memory still :
  'A boy's will is the wind's will,
And the thoughts of youth are long, long thoughts.'

" I remember the sea-fight far away,
  How it thundered o'er the tide !
And the dead captains as they lay
In their graves, o'erlooking the tranquil bay,
  Where they in battle died.
    And the sound of that mournful song
    Goes through me with a thrill :
  'A boy's will is the wind's will,
And the thoughts of youth are long, long thoughts."

In the same poem Longfellow speaks of the

  " Gleams and glooms that dart
Across the school-boy's brain."

The first school which he attended was a child's school,
kept on Spring Street by a dame known in the New England vernacular as Marm Fellows. Later he went to the
town school in Love Lane, now Centre Street, for a short
time, and then to the private school of Nathaniel H. Carter,
in a little one-story house on the west side of Preble Street,
now Congress. He was prepared for college at the Portland Academy, which had for masters the same Mr. Carter
and Mr. Bezaleel Cushman, who subsequently was editor of
the *New York Evening Post*. An usher, also, in the school
was Mr. Jacob Abbott, who afterward became famous as a
teacher and writer of books for children. His amiable and
indulgent manner remained in the recollection of his pupil.

The promise of his life was fulfilled a little in those earliest days. Ten miles from Portland is the old Longfellow homestead at Gorham, and thither the boy was wont to go. In later life he speaks of "my pleasant recollections of Gorham, the beautiful village, the elms, the farms. the pastures scented with pennyroyal, and the days of my boyhood, that have a perfume sweeter than field or flower." Here it was, perhaps, or in Deering Woods, that he had those early dreams to which he refers in the *Prelude* which opens his first published volume : —

> "And dreams of that which cannot die,
>   Bright visions, came to me,
> As lapped in thought I used to lie,
> And gaze into the summer sky,
> Where the sailing clouds went by,
>   Like ships upon the sea;

> "Dreams that the soul of youth engage
>   Ere Fancy has been quelled:
> Old legends of the monkish page,
> Traditions of the saint and sage,
> Tales that have the rime of age,
>   And chronicles of eld."

While he was still a school-boy he had begun to write and to print his poems. His first published poem was on *Lovell's Fight.* His experience in the publication was recalled by him once, in a conversation with a younger poet, William Winter. He had dropped the manuscript with fear and trembling into the editor's box at the office of a weekly newspaper in Portland. When the next issue of the paper appeared the boy looked eagerly. but in vain, for his verses. "But I had another copy," he said, "and I immediately sent it to the rival weekly, and the next week it was published. I have never since had such a thrill of delight over any of my publications;" and he told how he had bought a copy of the paper, still damp from the press, and walked with it into a by-street of the town, where he opened it, and found his poem actually printed.

He was ready for college when he was fourteen, and his father entered him at Bowdoin, but for some reason he passed the greater part of his Freshman year at home. His college life was one which increased the expectation of his friends. One of his teachers in college, the late venerable Professor A. S. Packard, once gave his reminiscences of the poet, who entered with his brother Stephen. "He was," says Professor Packard, "an attractive youth, with auburn locks, clear, fresh, blooming complexion, and, as might be presumed, of well-bred manners and bearing."

During his college life he contributed to the periodicals of the day. The most important of these, in a literary point of view, was the *United States Literary Gazette*, which was published simultaneously in New York and Boston. It was founded by Theophilus Parsons. To this periodical Longfellow contributed seventeen poems; the first five included under the division *Earlier Poems*, in his collected writings, were among the seventeen. Fourteen of Longfellow's poems contributed to the *Literary Gazette* were included in a little volume published in 1826, under the title of *Miscellaneous Poems selected from the United States Literary Gazette*, and one of these was *The Hymn of the Moravian Nuns*, which has always remained a favorite. In 1872 a friend brought from England Coleridge's inkstand, which he gave to Mr. Longfellow, who, in acknowledging the gift, wrote: —

"This memento of the poet recalls to my recollection that Theophilus Parsons, subsequently eminent in Massachusetts jurisprudence, paid me for a dozen of my early pieces that appeared in his *United States Literary Gazette* with a copy of Coleridge's poems, which I still have in my possession. Mr. Bryant contributed the *Forest Hymn*, *The Old Man's Funeral*, and many other poems to the same periodical, and thought he was well paid by receiving two dollars apiece; a price, by the way, which he himself placed upon the poems, and at least double the amount of my

honorarium.   Truly, times have changed with us *littéra-
teurs* during the last half century."

Longfellow graduated second in his class, and the class
was one having a number of men of singular ability.   It
would have been a great class in any college which held
Longfellow and Hawthorne, but this had also George B.
Cheever and Jonathan Cilley, a young man of great promise, who died in early manhood, and John S. C. Abbott.
Fifty years after graduation the surviving members met at
Brunswick, and Longfellow celebrated the occasion by his
noble *Morituri Salutamus*.

II.

Near the close of his college course an event took place
in the order of academic life which had an interesting influence on the poet's career.   The story is told by his class-
mate Abbott: " Mr. Longfellow studied Horace with great
enthusiasm.   There was one of his odes which he particularly admired.   He had made himself as familiar with it as
if it were written in his own mother tongue, and had translated it into his own glowing verse, which rivalled in melody
the diction of Horace.   There was at that time residing in
Brunswick a very distinguished lawyer by the name of Benjamin Orr.   Being a fine classical scholar, Horace was his
pocket companion, from whose pages he daily read.   He
was, as one of the Trustees of Bowdoin College, accustomed
to attend the annual examinations of the classes in the
classics.   In consequence of his accurate scholarship he was
greatly dreaded by the students.   The ode which pleased
young Henry Longfellow so much was also one of his favor-
ites.   It so happened that he called upon Longfellow to
translate that ode at, I think, our Senior examination.   The
translation was fluent and beautiful.   Mr. Orr was charmed,
and eagerly inquired the name of the brilliant scholar.
Soon after this the trustees of the college met to choose a
professor of modern languages.   Mr. Orr, whose voice was

potent in that board, said, " Why, Mr. Longfellow is your man. He is an admirable classical scholar. I have seldom heard anything more beautiful than his version of one of the most difficult odes of Horace."

The poet was but nineteen when the appointment was made, and the confidence which elder men had in him is more noticeable since the professorship to which he was called was a new one, and there were few, if any, precedents in other colleges to determine its character. At the time when the appointment came to him Longfellow was reading law in his father's office, but this was probably only incidental to his larger interest in literature. At any rate he accepted at once the offer made to him, and went to Europe to qualify himself for the position by study and travel.

He remained away three years and a half, and returned to enter upon his college duties in the fall of 1829. He had spent his time of preparation in England, France, Germany, Spain, and Italy, and had laid the foundation of that liberal knowledge of modern European literature which served him in such good stead throughout his life. His journey did more than this for him. It gave him the large background to his thoughts which served to bring out clearly the deeper purposes of life. In the glowing and affectionate dedication to Longfellow by George Washington Greene of his life of his grandfather, General Greene, there is a distinct reference to this period of the poet's life.

" Thirty-nine years ago this month of April," he writes in April, 1867, " you and I were together at Naples, wandering up and down amid the wonders of that historical city, and consciously in some things, and unconsciously in others, laying up those precious associations which are youth's best preparation for age. We were young then, with life all before us; and, in the midst of the records of a great past, our thoughts would still turn to our own future. Yet even in looking forward they caught the coloring of that past, making things bright to our eyes which, from a purely American point of view, would have worn a different aspect. From then till now the spell of those days has been upon us.

"One day — I shall never forget it — we returned at sunset from a long afternoon amid the statues and relics of the Museo Borbonico. Evening was coming on, with a sweet promise of the stars: and our minds and hearts were so full that we could not think of shutting ourselves up in our rooms, or of mingling with the crowd on the Toledo. We wanted to be alone, and yet to feel that there was life all around us. We went up to the flat roof of the house, where, as we walked, we could look down into the crowded street, and out upon the wonderful bay, and across the bay to Ischia and Capri and Sorrento, and over the house-tops and villas and vineyards to Vesuvius. . . . And over all, with a thrill like that of solemn music, fell the splendor of the Italian sunset.

"We talked and mused by turns, till the twilight deepened and the stars came forth to mingle their mysterious influences with the overmastering magic of the scene. It was then that you unfolded to me your plans of life, and showed me from what 'deep cisterns' you had already learned to draw. From that day the office of literature took a new place in my thoughts. I felt its forming power as I had never felt it before, and began to look with a calm resignation upon its trials, and with true appreciation upon its rewards."

It is interesting, as one thinks of Longfellow in his youth, and again in the splendor of his age, to turn to the words with which he closes the record of his first journey: —

"My pilgrimage is ended. I have come home to rest: and recording the time past, I have fulfilled these things, and written them in this book, as it would come into my mind, — for the most part, when the duties of the day were over, and the world around me was hushed in sleep. . . .

The morning watches have begun. And as I write the melancholy thought intrudes upon me, To what end is all this toil? Of what avail these midnight vigils? Dost thou covet fame? Vain dreamer! A few brief days, and what will the busy world know of thee?" He is described at this time as "full of the ardor excited by classical pursuits. He had sunny locks, a fresh complexion, and clear blue eyes, with all the indications of a joyous temperament."

He entered upon his work as professor with such spirit that he began very early to draw students to Bowdoin. Two years after entering upon his new duties, he was married to Mary Storer Potter, daughter of Hon. Barrett Potter and Anne (Storer) Potter, of Portland. Judge Potter was a man of strong character, and his daughter, by the testimony of those who knew her, was both strong in her intellectual nature and of rare beauty of person. It is thought that the reference is to her in the verses *Footsteps of Angels*, where the poet, seeing in a reverie the forms of departed friends, sings: —

" And with them the Being Beauteous
    Who unto my youth was given,
  More than all things else to love me,
    And is now a saint in heaven.

" With a slow and noiseless footstep
    Comes that messenger divine,
  Takes the vacant chair beside me,
    Lays her gentle hand in mine.

" And she sits and gazes at me
    With those deep and tender eyes,
  Like the stars, so still and saint-like,
    Looking downward from the skies."

Mr. Longfellow held his professorship at Bowdoin for five years, and during this time put forth his first formal publications. The earliest book with which he had to do was *Elements of French Grammar*, translated from the

French of C. F. L'Homond. and published in 1830.   Other works, edited or translated by him. and having direct reference to his occupation as a professor of modern languages and literature. appeared during these five years.   The subjects of his more purely literary productions during this period were also closely connected with his profession.   He published articles in the *North American Review* on the *Origin and Progress of the French Language.* a *Defence of Poetry.* on the *History of the Italian Language and Dialects,* on *Spanish Language and Literature,* on *Old English Romances.* and on *Spanish Devotional and Moral Poetry.*   In 1833 he took this last essay, and attaching to it a translation of Manrique's *Coplas,* and of some sonnets by Lope de Vega and others, produced a volume entitled *Coplas de Manrique,* which may be regarded as his first purely literary venture in book form.   His name was placed on the title-page with his title as professor. and the book was published by Allen & Ticknor. predecessors of the present publishers of his works.

Meanwhile he was beginning to make use of the abundant material which he had gathered during his European sojourn, in the form of sketches of travel and little romances drawn from legendary lore.   He began in *The New England Magazine.* a periodical long since dead. a series of papers under the title *The Schoolmaster.* but discontinued them after a few numbers and used some of this material and much more in his first considerable book. *Outre-Mer.*

This book appeared at first with no name attached, but it was probably well known who wrote it; and when the second part appeared. shortly afterward. Professor Longfellow's name was openly connected with it.   The last three chapters of *The Schoolmaster* were not reprinted. and the serial was not resumed, perhaps because the author preferred the more satisfactory and more dignified appearance in book form.   A prior publication in a magazine was more likely to obscure a book then than now. It is not impossible that the slight conception of a schoolmaster was reserved, also, for future use in the tale of *Kavanagh*.

His work as an author and that as a professor were substantially one. "He proved himself," says one of his contemporaries at Bowdoin, "a teacher who never wearied of his work, who won by his gentle grace, and commanded respect by his self-respect and his respect for his office." He assumed the duties of librarian, also, and his work was comprehensively literary. He was twenty-six years old, and had made a positive place in literature.

III.

In a letter dated Boston, January 5, 1835, Mr. George Ticknor, then Professor of the French and Spanish Languages and of Belles Lettres at Harvard College, wrote as follows to his friend, C. S. Daveis, of Portland: "Besides wishing you a happy New Year, I have a word to say about myself. I have substantially resigned my place at Cambridge, and Longfellow is appointed substantially to fill it. I say *substantially*, because he is to pass a year or more in Germany and the North of Europe, and I am to continue in the place till he returns, which will be in a year from next Commencement, or thereabouts."

The transfer from Bowdoin to Harvard grew out of the increasing reputation of the young professor, and in taking another journey to Europe he was carrying forward the same spirit of thorough preparation, and was completing the survey of European languages and literature, by making acquaintance with those parts unvisited in his former residence abroad. His eighteen months of travel and study were very productive, but they were shadowed by the death of his wife, who was taken ill at Rotterdam, and died there November 29, 1835. The record of his life during this time is partially disclosed in the pages of *Hyperion*, and the mournful character of its early chapters may well be

taken as echoing the temper in which he pursued his soli-
tary studies.

He returned to America in November, 1836, and after
a short visit to his home in Portland he entered upon his
new work at Cambridge. The house which is so identified
with Longfellow's life was his home from the time he came
to Cambridge until his death, although it was not till 1843
that he became actual owner of it. The ample, dignified
mansion on Brattle Street has a generous surrounding of
green fields, and a clear outlook across meadows to the
winding Charles and the gentle hills beyond, but in 1836
it was even more rural in its position. The history of the
house carries it back to the days of the rich Tory mer-
chants, who were so loath to abandon the ease and dignity
of the province for the anxieties and levelling of an inde-
pendence of England. It was built by John Vassall in
1759, as a home for himself and his bride, who was a sister
of the last royal lieutenant-governor of the province. At
the outbreak of the Revolution Vassall fled to London, and
the house passed into the hands of the provincial government. When soldiers flocked to Cambridge, after the Lex-
ington and Concord fight, it was used by a battalion of
Colonel John Glover's regiment of Marblehead fishermen.
They held it but a short time, for upon Washington's arrival in Cambridge the house, as the most commodious in
the place, was made ready for the general's headquarters.
Here Washington and his military family remained during
the siege of Boston.

Upon the transfer of military movements southward,
Nathaniel Tracy, of Newburyport, who had grown rich by
privateering, bought the estate : but his wealth vanished
almost as rapidly as it was acquired, and in 1786 the place
was sold to Thomas Russell, the first president of the United
States Branch Bank ; and he in his turn sold it in 1792
to Andrew Craigie, who had been apothecary-general to
the Continental Army, and had amassed a fortune in that

CRAIGIE HOUSE, CAMBRIDGE

office. He became embarrassed in his affairs, and when he died his widow, who continued to live there, drew her income in part from the lease of rooms in her house to college officers and others. Mr. Sparks went there to live, and was at work upon his edition of the life and writings of Washington in the very room occupied by the general. Hither also came Dr. Edward Everett, and here lived and worked Dr. Joseph E. Worcester, the lexicographer.

The story is told that when Mr. Longfellow knocked at the door and asked the stately old lady if she would receive him as a lodger, she demurred.

" I am sorry to tell you," she said, "that I never have students to live with me."

" But I am not a student," he replied. " I am a professor in the University."

" A professor?" She looked curiously at one so like most students in appearance.

" I am Professor Longfellow," he said.

" If you are the author of *Outre-Mer*, then you can come," said the old lady, and proceeded to show him her house. She led him up the broad staircase, and, proud of the historic mansion, opened one spacious room after another, only to close the door of each, saying, " You cannot have that," until at length she led him into the southeast corner room of the second story. " This was General Washington's chamber," she said ; " you may have this." And here he gladly set up his home.

Old Madam Craigie continued to live in the house until her death. On one occasion her poet lodger, entering her parlor in the morning, found her sitting by the open window, through which innumerable canker-worms had crawled from the trees they were devouring outside. They had fastened themselves to her dress, and hung in little writhing festoons from the white turban on her head. Her visitor, surprised and shocked, asked if he could do nothing to destroy the worms. Raising her eyes from the book which she sat calmly reading, she said in tones of solemn rebuke, "Young man, have not our fellow-worms as good a right to live as we?" Dr. Worcester bought the estate, and afterward sold it to Mr. Longfellow.

He spent seventeen years in Cambridge as professor, and he carried the title the rest of his days. It has not been customary of late years to associate Mr. Longfellow with academic life, but while he was engaged in it he gave himself to it with great assiduity. Under Mr. Ticknor's management, the modern languages and literature at Harvard had been erected into a department, with four foreigners for teachers, all being directed and supervised by the professor in charge. Something of the nature of this department plan, which was an innovation upon the customary college method, may be gathered from the letter of Mr. Ticknor already quoted, in which he announced the election of Mr. Longfellow. "Within the limits of the department," he writes, "I have entirely broken up the division of classes, established fully the principle and practice of progress according to proficiency, and introduced a system of voluntary study, which for several years has embraced from one hundred and forty to one hundred and sixty students; so that we have relied hardly at all on college discipline, as it is called, but almost entirely on the good dispositions of the young men and their desire to learn."

The traditions of this department were carried forward by Mr. Longfellow, as may be seen by an animated letter of reminiscences, written in 1881 by Rev. Edward Everett Hale, who was one of his students: —

"I was so fortunate as to be in the first 'section,' which Mr. Longfellow instructed personally when he came to Cambridge in 1836. Perhaps I best illustrate the method of his instruction when I say that I think every man in that section would now say that he was on intimate terms with Mr. Longfellow. We are all near sixty now, but I think that every one of the section would expect to have Mr. Longfellow recognize him, and would enter into familiar talk with him if they met. From the first he chose to take with us the relation of a personal friend a few years older than we were.

"As it happened, the regular recitation rooms of the college were all in use, and indeed I think he was hardly expected to teach any language at all. He was to oversee the department and to lecture. But he seemed to teach us German for the love of it : I know I thought he did, and till now it never occurred to me to ask whether it were a part of his regular duty. Any way, we did not meet him in one of the rather dingy 'recitation rooms,' but in a sort of parlor, carpeted, hung with pictures, and otherwise handsomely furnished, which was, I believe, called 'the Corporation Room.' We sat round a mahogany table, which was reported to be meant for the dinners of the trustees, and the whole affair had the aspect of a friendly gathering in a private house, in which the study of German was the amusement of the occasion. These accidental surroundings of the place characterize well enough the whole proceeding.

"He began with familiar ballads, read them to us, and made us read them to him. Of course we soon committed them to memory without meaning to, and I think this was probably part of his theory. At the same time we were learning the paradigms by rote. But we never studied the grammar except to learn them, nor do I know to this hour what are the contents of half the pages in the regular German grammars.

"This was quite too good to last ; for his regular duty was the oversight of five or more instructors, who were teaching French, German, Italian, Spanish, and Portuguese to two or three hundred undergraduates. All these gentlemen were of European birth, and you know how undergraduates are apt to fare with such men. Mr. Longfellow had a real administration of the whole department. His title was 'Smith Professor of Modern Literature,' but we always called him 'the Head,' because he was head of the department. We never knew when he might look in on a recitation and virtually conduct it. We were delighted to have him come. Any slipshod work of some poor wretch from France, who was tormented by wild-cat Sophomores, would be made straight and decorous and all right. We all knew he was a poet, and were proud to have him in the college, but at the same time we respected him as a man of affairs.

" Besides this, he lectured on authors or more general subjects. I think attendance was voluntary, but I know we never missed a lecture. I have full notes of his lectures on Dante's *Divina Commedia*, which confirm my recollections, namely, that he read the whole to us in English, and explained whatever he thought needed comment. I have often referred to these notes since. And though I suppose he included all that he thought worth while in his notes to his translation of Dante, I know that until that was published I could find no such reservoir of comment on the poem."

Another of his pupils, T. W. Higginson, in recalling the days of Longfellow's professorship, writes : " In respect of courtesy his manners quite anticipated the present time, and were a marked advance upon the merely pedagogical relation which then prevailed. He was one of the few professors who then addressed his pupils as 'Mr.;' his tone to them, though not paternal or brotherly, was always gentlemanly. On one occasion, during an abortive movement toward rebellion, some of the elder professors tried in vain to obtain a hearing from a crowd of angry students collected in the college yard; but when Longfellow spoke, there was a hush, and the word went round, 'Let us hear Professor Longfellow, for he always treats us as gentlemen.' As an instructor he was clear, suggestive, and encouraging ; his lectures on the great French writers were admirable, and his facility in equivalent phrases was of great use to his pupils and elevated their standard of translation. He was scrupulously faithful to his duties, and even went through the exhausting process of marking French exercises with exemplary patience. Besides his own classes in Molière, Racine, and other poets, he had the general supervision of his department, which included subordinate teachers in French, Spanish, Italian, and German. All these were under his authority, and he doubtless had the selection of all appointees. There was probably no college in the United States which had so large a corps of instructors in the modern languages as had Harvard at that time."

With the regular, methodical habits indicated in the foregoing reminiscences, the professor found place for the *littérateur* and poet. Contributions to the *North American* " were continued," and it is to be noted that one of these was a hearty recognition of Hawthorne's *Twice - Told Tales*, which appeared in 1837, and needed at the time all the encouragement which appreciative minds could give. How much pleasure it gave to Hawthorne may be read in the letter which the story-teller was moved to write to the critic : —

SALEM, *June* 19, 1837.

DEAR LONGFELLOW, — I have to-day received and read with huge delight your review of Hawthorne's *Twice-Told Tales.* I frankly own that I was not without hopes that you would do this kind office for the book ; though I could not have anticipated how very kindly it would be done. Whether or no the public will agree to the praise which you bestow on me, there are at least five persons who think you the most sagacious critic on earth, namely, my mother and two sisters, my old maiden aunt, and finally the strongest believer of the whole five, my own self. If I doubt the sincerity and correctness of any of my critics, it shall be of those who censure me. Hard would be the lot of a poor scribbler, if he may not have this privilege. . . .

Very sincerely yours,
NATH. HAWTHORNE.

Other papers of this period were articles on *Tegnér's*

Frithiof's Saga and *Anglo-Saxon Literature*, indicative of his scholastic work.

IV.

As *Outre-Mer* was, in some ways the report of his first journey to Europe, so *Hyperion* stands as expressive of his second. *Outre-Mer* is a record of travel, continuous in its geographical outline, but separated from ordinary itineraries by noting less the personal accidents of the traveller than the poetic and romantic scenes which, whether of the present or the past, marked the journey and transformed it into the pilgrimage of a devotee to art. In *Hyperion* a more deliberate romance is intended, but the lights and shades of the story are heightened or deepened by the passages of travel and study, which form the background from which the human figures are relieved. It is interesting to observe how, as the writer was more withdrawn from the actual Europe of his eyes, he used the Europe of his memory and imagination to wait upon the movements of a profounder study, the adventures of a human soul. These two books and the occasional critical papers are characterized by a strong consciousness of literary art. Life seems always to suggest a book or a picture, and nature is always viewed in its immediate relation to form and color. There is a singular discovery of the Old World, and while European writers like Châteaubriand, for example, were turning to America for new and unworn images, Longfellow, reflecting the awaking desire for the enduring forms of art which his countrymen were showing, eagerly disclosed the treasures to which the owners seemed almost indifferent. It is difficult to measure the influence which his broad, catholic taste and his refined choice of subjects have had upon American culture through the medium of these works, and that large body of his poetry which draws an inspiration from foreign life.

Hyperion at once became a general favorite. Barry Cornwall is said to have read it through once a year for the sake of its style. It is so faithful in its descriptions that it still serves as a companion to travellers on the Rhine, and is read at Heidelberg and elsewhere somewhat as Byron used to be read in Switzerland and Italy. It contains some translations also of German verse, which by their musical form obtained at once a popularity aside from the prose romance.

The same year, 1839, which saw the publication of *Hyperion* saw also the appearance of Longfellow's first volume given wholly to verse, a thin book entitled *Voices of the Night*. He had been contributing poems from time to time to the *Knickerbocker Magazine*, and he now collected these, some of the earlier poems contributed to the *United States Literary Gazette*, the poetry in the volume of *Coplas de Manrique*, the verses contained in *Hyperion*, and other translations. The most famous poem in this collection was the *Psalm of Life*. It was written, we are told by Mr. Fields, on a bright summer morning in July, 1838, as the poet sat at a small table between two windows, in the corner of his chamber. He kept it unpublished for some time, since it had a very close connection in his own mind with the troubles through which he had lately passed.

In 1841 the next volume of poems was issued, under the title of *Ballads and other Poems*, — a title still preserved in a division of his collected poems. It may be said to contain more of his famous short poems than any other volume which he issued, for it opens with *The Skeleton in Armor*; it holds *The Wreck of the Hesperus*, *The Village Blacksmith*, *The Rainy Day*, *To the River Charles*, *Maidenhood*, and *Excelsior*. In the notes to his poems Mr. Longfellow has himself related the slight incidents which led to the writing of *The Skeleton in Armor*.

A letter from Mr. Longfellow to Mr. Charles Lanman

gives an interesting account of the circumstances attending the production of *The Wreck of the Hesperus* : —

CAMBRIDGE, *November* 24, 1871.

MY DEAR SIR, — Last night I had the pleasure of receiving your friendly letter and the beautiful pictures that came with it, and I thank you cordially for the welcome gift and the kind remembrance that prompted it. They are both very interesting to me ; particularly the Reef of Norman's Woe. What you say of the ballad is also very gratifying, and induces me to send you in return a bit of autobiography.

Looking over a journal for 1839, a few days ago, I found the following entries : —

" December 17. — News of shipwrecks, horrible, on the coast. Forty bodies washed ashore near Gloucester. One woman lashed to a piece of wreck. There is a reef called Norman's Woe, where many of these took place. Among others the schooner Hesperus. Also, the Seaflower, on Black Rock. I will write a ballad on this.

" December 30. — Wrote last evening a notice of Allston's poems, after which sat till 1 o'clock by the fire, smoking ; when suddenly it came into my head to write the Ballad of the Schooner Hesperus, which I accordingly did. Then went to bed, but could not sleep. New thoughts were running in my mind, and I got up to add them to the Ballad. It was 3 by the clock."

All this is of no importance but to myself. However, I like sometimes to recall the circumstances under which a poem was written, and as you express a liking for this one it may perhaps interest you to know why and when and how it came into existence. I had quite forgotten about its first publication ; but I find a letter from Park Benjamin, dated January 7, 1840, beginning (you will recognize his style) as follows : —

" Your ballad, *The Wreck of The Hesperus*, is grand. Inclosed are twenty-five dollars (the sum you mentioned) for it, paid by the proprietors of ' The New World,' in which glorious paper it will resplendently coruscate on Saturday next."

Pardon this gossip, and believe me, with renewed thanks, yours faithfully,

HENRY W. LONGFELLOW.

The word *excelsior* happened to catch his eye one evening as he was reading a bit of newspaper, and his mind began to kindle over the suggestion of the word. He took the nearest scrap of paper, which happened to be a letter from Charles Sumner, and wrote the verses with corrections on the back. The scrap is still preserved and shown at the library of Harvard University. A pretty story is told of the fortunes of one of the poems in the volume, the well-known *Maidenhood*. Once when it was printed in an illustrated paper, it fell into the hands of a poor woman living in a lonely cabin in a sterile portion of the Northwest. She had papered the walls of her cabin with the journals which a friend had sent her, and this poem with its picture was upon the wall by her table. Here, as she stood at her bread-making or ironing, day after day, she gazed at the picture and read the poem until, by long brooding over it, she understood it and absorbed it as people rarely possess the words they read. The friend who sent her the papers was himself a man of letters, and coming afterward to see her in her loneliness, stood amazed and humbled as she talked to him artlessly about the poem, and disclosed the depths of her intelligence of its beauty and thought.

In 1842 he paid a third visit to Europe. It was on his return voyage in October that he wrote the *Poems on Slavery* which made his next volume, and formed his contribution to the discussion which was then engrossing so much of the thought of the country.

In July, 1843, he married Miss Fanny Appleton, daughter of the late Nathan Appleton, of Boston, a lady of noble bearing, of great beauty of person and dignity of character, whom he had met on his recent journey in Europe. By her he had two sons and three daughters. Mrs. Longfellow died July 9, 1861, under circumstances which caused a terrible shock. She had been amusing her children with some seals which she made, when some of the burning wax fell upon her light summer dress, and

before help could be given she had received severe burns,
from which she died in a few hours. The shock to the
poet was so great that for a time it seemed as if reason
itself was in danger; but the firmness and calmness of
his nature reasserted itself, and he slowly came back to his
singing. His friends were wont to observe, however, his
increased signs of age and the greater silence of his life.
"I have never heard him make but one allusion to the
great grief of his life," said an intimate friend. "We
were speaking of Schiller's fine poem, 'The Ring of Poly-
crates.' He said, 'It was just so with me. I was too
happy. I might fancy the gods envied me, if I could
fancy heathen gods.'"

To return to his publications in the order of their appearance. *The Spanish Student* came out in 1843, and
in 1845 he edited a little collection of poems called *The
Waif.* In the same year, also, he made the important collection known as *The Poets and Poetry of Europe,* containing biographical and critical sketches, with translations
by various English poets, his own contribution being considerable. In 1846 appeared *The Belfry of Bruges and
other Poems,* and the next year came *Evangeline.*

Two years later, in 1849, appeared Mr. Longfellow's
latest prose work, *Kavanagh,* a tale of New England life,
and in 1850 a new volume of poems, entitled *The Seaside
and the Fireside.* The dedication of this volume, addressed to no one name, is a graceful acknowledgment of
the multitudinous responses which he was now receiving.
"Thanks," he says, —

> "Thanks for the sympathies that ye have shown!
>   Thanks for each kindly word, each silent token,
> That teaches me, when seeming most alone,
>   Friends are around us, though no word be spoken.
>
> "Kind messages, that pass from land to land;
>   Kind letters, that betray the heart's deep history,
> In which we feel the pressure of a hand, —
>   One touch of fire, — and all the rest is mystery!"

And the *Dedication* closes with words which had a truly prophetic meaning : —

> " Therefore I hope, as no unwelcome guest,
>   At your warm fireside, when the lamps are lighted,
> To have my place reserved among the rest,
>   Nor stand as one unsought and uninvited ! "

The longest poem in the collection was *The Building of the Ship*, — " that admirably constructed poem," as Dr. Holmes says, " beginning with the literal description, passing into the higher region of sentiment by the most natural of transitions, and ending with the noble climax,

> " ' Thou too sail on, O Ship of State,'

which has become the classical expression of patriotic emotion." It would be curious if it should prove that the ode of Horace, the translation of which led to Mr. Longfellow's appointment to a professorship at Bowdoin, was that one beginning —

> " O navis referent in mare te novi,"

which the poet so nobly repeated in higher strains at the close of *The Building of the Ship.* Mr. Noah Brooks, in a paper on " Lincoln's Imagination," which he contributed to *Scribner's Monthly* (August, 1879), mentions that he found the President one day attracted by these closing stanzas, which were quoted in a political speech. " Knowing the whole poem," he adds, " as one of my early exercises in recitation, I began, at his request, with the description of the launch of the ship, and repeated it to the end. As he listened to the last lines, —

> " ' Our hearts, our hopes, are all with thee,
>   Our hearts, our hopes, our prayers, our tears,
>   Our faith triumphant o'er our fears,
>   Are all with thee, — are all with thee ! '

his eyes filled with tears, and his cheeks were wet. He did not speak for some minutes, but finally said with simplicity. ' It is a wonderful gift to be able to stir men like that.' "

V.

The critics had complained of the European flavor of Mr. Longfellow's verse. He was steadily keeping on his way, however, expressing his nature honestly, and finding a noble delivery in such national poems as *The Building of the Ship.*

It is noticeable how much more fully the tide of his poetry set in the direction of America after the publication of *Evangeline :* while *The Golden Legend* was published in 1851, and is perhaps the most perfect expression of the Old World in his verse. *The Song of Hiawatha* appeared in 1855, and awakened an enthusiasm which was unexampled in the history of his literary career.

The story is told that in the summer of 1857 acting Governor Stanton, of Kansas, paid a visit to the citizens of Lawrence, in that State. After partaking of the hospitalities shown him by Governor Robinson, he addressed, by request, a crowd of some five hundred free-state men, who did not hesitate to manifest their disapprobation at such portions of his speech as did not accord with their peculiar political views. At the close of his speech Mr. Stanton pictured in glowing language the Indian tradition of Hiawatha, of the "peace pipe" shaped and fashioned by Gitche Manito, and by which he called tribes of men together, closing with the lines, —

> " I am weary of your quarrels,
> Weary of your wars and bloodshed,
> Weary of your prayers for vengeance,
> Of your wranglings and dissensions ;
> All your strength is in your union,
> All your danger is in discord ;
> Therefore be at peace henceforward,
> And as brothers live together."

The aptness of the quotation from so favorite a poem acted

like a charm for the time in pacifying the crowd, who applauded vociferously.

Innumerable discussions arose over the faithfulness of the poem to Indian traditions, but the most renowned Indian scholars supported the claims of the poem to truthfulness, and the liquid names passed at once into common use. It may fairly be said that by this work a popularity was given to Indian names which did much to preserve them from disuse as titles to rivers, mountains, and districts.

The Courtship of Miles Standish appeared in 1858, and the volume bearing this title contained also a number of short poems, under the collective title *Birds of Passage.* *The Atlantic Monthly* had been established the year before, and in the first number Mr. Longfellow published his poem *Santa Filomena.* He became a very frequent contributor, and some of the poems in this volume were those which had thus far appeared in *The Atlantic.* Indeed, after this date, his smaller volumes of original verse were for the most part collections from time to time of poems which were first printed in that magazine. In the following year the poet received the degree of Doctor of Laws from Harvard.

In the fall of 1863 was published *Tales of a Wayside Inn,* with a few poems added under the title *Birds of Passage, Flight the Second.* The Tales constitute the division known as the First Day, for the volume as now published contains also two other parts. The *Prelude* to this first part, introducing the characters who share in the festivities of the Inn, has always been a favorite; and the several personages have been identified with more or less confidence, the Inn itself being the old Howe Tavern, which still stands by the turnpike which runs through Sudbury, in Massachusetts: the landlord is easily said to stand for Lyman Howe; the theologian for Professor Treadwell, the physicist, who was also an unprofessional student of theol-

ogy; the poet for T. W. Parsons, the musician for Ole
Bull, the student for Henry Wales, and the Sicilian for
Luigi Monti. The original, if there was one, of the Span-
ish Jew is not known.

Flower-de-Luce was the title of a small volume of poems
published in 1867, and the same year appeared the first
of the three volumes containing the poet's translation of
Dante, a work which was completed by the press in 1872.
One of his friends states that his translation of the *Inferno*
"was the result of ten minutes' daily work at a standing
desk in his library, while his coffee was reaching the boil-
ing point on his breakfast table." As he was an orderly
man, and like all highly organized natures set a high value
on time, this may well have been; but the final result was
obtained only after a long and careful consideration, in
which the poet invited the aid of Mr. Lowell, Professor
Norton, Mr. Howells, and other Italian scholars, who met
with him in a little club for the discussion of the work.

In May, 1868, Mr. Longfellow again visited Europe
with his family, and, going now with the accumulating
honors of his eminent career, his presence was the occasion
there of marked homage. Especially was this true in England, where he received abundant social and civic honors.
The University of Cambridge conferred on him the degree
of Doctor of Laws, and Oxford gave him the title of
Doctor of Civil Law the next year. An English reporter
describes him as he appeared at Cambridge in the scarlet
robes of an academic dignitary: —

"The face was one which, I think, would have caught the
spectator's glance even if his attention had not been called
to it by the cheers which greeted Longfellow's appearance
in the robes of an LL. D. Long white silken hair and a
beard of patriarchal length and whiteness inclosed a young,
fresh-colored countenance, with fine-cut features and deep-
sunken eyes, overshadowed by massive black eyebrows.
Looking at him, you had the feeling that the white head of

hair and beard were a mask put on to conceal a young man's face; and that if the poet chose he could throw off the disguise, and appear as a man in the prime and bloom of life."

VI.

Mr. Longfellow returned to his home in the fall of 1869. During his absence *The New England Tragedies* had been published, and in 1872 came out *The Divine Tragedy.* At the same time the poet published his *Christus,* which consists of *The Divine Tragedy, The Golden Legend,* and *The New England Tragedies,* as a consecutive trilogy, and it is to be regarded as the poet's most serious and profound undertaking. In the same year appeared also *Three Books of Song,* which contained the Second Day of *Tales of a Wayside Inn, Judas Maccabæus,* and a number of translations. In 1874 was published *Aftermath,* which comprised the completion of *Tales of a Wayside Inn* and the *Third Flight of Birds of Passage. The Masque of Pandora* and other poems followed in 1875.

This volume contained the poem *Morituri Salutamus,* read by the poet at the gathering of his classmates upon the fiftieth anniversary of graduation at Bowdoin. The occasion was one of singular interest, and the fact that the poet had never publicly recited one of his poems except in the case of the Phi Beta Kappa poem at Harvard in 1833, gave a special value to the services in the plain church building at Brunswick. He expressed his relief when he found that he could read his poem from the pulpit, for, as he said, "Let me cover myself as much as possible; I wish it might be entirely." In the same volume was *The Hanging of the Crane,* the delightful domestic poem which had been previously issued with abundant illustrations the year before, after it had been first printed in *The New York Ledger,* the poet receiving for its publication there the unprecedented sum of four thousand dollars. *The*

Masque of Pandora was adapted for the stage and set to music by Alfred Cellier, and brought out at the Boston Theatre in 1881.

Shortly after the publication of this volume there began to appear a series of volumes, edited by Mr. Longfellow, entitled *Poems of Places*, which were published at intervals during the next four years, and extended to thirty-one volumes; the work of sifting and arranging these poems gave him an agreeable occupation, for he was always at home in the best poetry of the world. While the series was in progress he issued, in 1878, *Kéramos and other Poems*, which gathered up the poems which he had been publishing the past three years. It is noticeable that in these later volumes the sonnet held a conspicuous place. Among these is the touching one entitled *A Nameless Grave*, of which the origin is told by Mrs. Applhia Howard : —

"I found in 1864, on a torn scrap of the Boston *Saturday Evening Gazette*, a description of a burying-ground in Newport News, where on the head-board of a soldier might be read the words 'A Union Soldier mustered out,' and this was the only inscription. The correspondent told the brief story very effectively, and, knowing Mr. Longfellow's intense patriotism and devotion to the Union, I thought it would impress him greatly. I knew also that the account would seem vital to him from the fact that his own son Charles was a Union soldier and severely wounded during the war.

"After carefully pasting the broken bits together on a bit of cardboard I sent it to Mr. Longfellow by Mr. [G. W.] Greene, who did not think Longfellow would use it, for he declared 'a poet could not write to order.' In a few days Mr. Longfellow acknowledged it by a letter, which I did not at all expect, as follows : —

"'In the writing of letters, more, perhaps, than in anything else, Shakespeare's words are true ; and

> ' " The flighty purpose never is o'ertook
>   Unless the deed go with it."

For this reason, the touching incident you have sent me
has not yet shaped itself poetically in my mind, as I hope
it some day will. Meanwhile, I thank you most sincerely
for bringing it to my notice, and I agree with you in thinking it very beautiful.' " It was ten years and more before
the sonnet was printed ; how long it may have lain in the
poet's drawer we do not know.

The last published volume was *Ultima Thule*, issued in
1880, and containing a few melodious verses. A singular
interest attaches to the volume. It is dedicated to his life-
long friend George Washington Greene, whose tender dedication to the poet of his life of his grandfather disclosed a
little of the poet's inner life also. It touches upon the
friendships of the poet, that for Bayard Taylor and for the
poet Dana, and it contains the lines *From my Arm-Chair*,
which have set a precious seal upon the poet's relation to
childhood. The origin of the poem is well known, but de-
serves to be repeated. The poem *The Village Blacksmith*
had been a great favorite, and visitors to Cambridge did not
fail to seek the spreading chestnut under which the smithy
once stood. The smithy disappeared several years ago ; but
the tree remained until 1876, when the city government,
with a prudent zeal which no remonstrance of the poet and
his friends could divert, ordered it to be cut down, on the
plea that its low branches endangered drivers upon high
loads passing upon the road beneath it.

The after-thought came to construct some memento of the
tree for the poet, and the result was the presentation, upon
the poet's seventy-second birthday, by the children of Cambridge, of a chair made from the wood of the tree. The
color is a dead black, the effect being produced by ebon-
izing the wood. The upholstering of the arms and the cushion is in green leather. The casters are glass balls set in
sockets. In the back of the chair is a circular piece of

carving, consisting of horse-chestnut leaves and blossoms. Horse-chestnut leaves and burrs are presented in varied combinations at other points.   Underneath the cushion is a brass plate, on which is the following inscription : —

To
THE AUTHOR
of
THE VILLAGE BLACKSMITH
This chair, made from the wood of the
spreading chestnut-tree,
is presented as
An expression of grateful regard and veneration
by
The Children of Cambridge,
who with their friends join in best wishes
and congratulations
on
This Anniversary,
February 27, 1879.

Around the seat, in raised German text, are the lines from the poem, —

> " And children coming home from school
>   Look in at the open door;
> And catch the burning sparks that fly
>   Like chaff from a threshing floor."

The poem *From my Arm-Chair* was the poet's response to the gift.   In 1880, when the city of Cambridge celebrated the two hundred and fiftieth anniversary of the founding of the town, December 28th, there was a children's festival in the morning at Sanders Theatre, and the chair stood prominently on the platform, where the thousand school-children gathered could see it.   The poem was read to them by Mr. Riddle, and, better than all, the poet himself came forward, to the surprise of all who knew how absolute was his silence on public occasions, and standing, the picture of beautiful old age, he spoke smilingly these few words to the delighted children : —

My dear Young Friends, — I do not rise to make an address to you, but to excuse myself from making one. I know the proverb says that he who excuses himself accuses himself, and I am willing on this occasion to accuse myself, for I feel very much as I suppose some of you do when you are suddenly called upon in your class-room, and are obliged to say that you are not prepared. I am glad to see your faces and to hear your voices. I am glad to have this opportunity of thanking you in prose, as I have already done in verse, for the beautiful present you made me some two years ago. Perhaps some of you have forgotten it, but I have not ; and I am afraid — yes, I am afraid — that fifty years hence, when you celebrate the three hundredth anniversary of this occasion, this day and all that belongs to it will have passed from your memory ; for an English philosopher has said that the ideas as well as children of our youth often die before us, and our minds represent to us those tombs to which we are approaching, where, though the brass and marble remain, yet the inscriptions are effaced by time, and the imagery moulders away.

The chair gave the children a proud feeling of proprietorship in the poet, and hundreds of little boys and girls presented themselves at the door of the famous house. None were ever turned away, and pleasant memories will linger in the minds of those who boldly asked for the poet's hospitality, unconscious of the tax which they laid upon him. A pleasant story is told by Luigi Monti, who had for many years been in the habit of dining with the poet every Saturday. One Christmas, as he was walking toward the house, he was accosted by a girl about twelve years old, who inquired where Mr. Longfellow lived. He told her it was some distance down the street, but if she would walk along with him he would show her. When they reached the gate, she said, —

"Do you think I can go into the yard ? "

"Oh, yes," said Signor Monti. "Do you see the room

on the left? That is where Martha Washington held her
receptions a hundred years ago. If you look at the windows on the right you will probably see a white-haired
gentleman reading a paper. Well, that will be Mr. Longfellow."

The child looked gratified and happy at the unexpected
pleasure of really seeing the man whose poems she said she
loved. As Signor Monti drew near the house he saw Mr.
Longfellow standing with his back against the window, his
head out of sight. When he went in, the kind-hearted
Italian said, —

"Do look out of the window and bow to that little girl,
who wants to see you very much."

"A little girl wants to see me very much? Where is
she?" He hastened to the door, and, beckoning with his
hand, called out, "Come here, little girl; come here, if you
want to see me." She came forward, and he took her hand
and asked her name. Then he kindly led her into the
house, showed her the old clock on the stairs, the children's
chair, and the various souvenirs which he had gathered.
This was but one little instance of many.

Indeed, it was not to children alone that he was kind.
Numberless were the acts of courtesy which he showed not
to the courteous only, but to those whom others would
have turned away. "Bores of all nations," says Mr. Norton, "especially of our own, persecuted him. His long-suf-
fering patience was a wonder to his friends. It was, in
truth, the sweetest charity. No man was ever before so
kind to these moral mendicants. One day I ventured to
remonstrate with him on his endurance of the persecutions
of one of the worst of the class, who to lack of modesty
added lack of honesty, — a wretched creature, — and when
I had done he looked at me with a pleasant, reproving,
humorous glance, and said, 'Charles, who would be kind to
him if I were not?' It was enough."

"I happened," says a writer, "to be often brought into

contact with a very intelligent but cynical and discontented laboring man, who never lost an opportunity of railing against the rich. To such men wealth and poverty are the only distinctions in life. In one of his denunciations I heard him say, ' I will make an exception of one rich man, and that is Mr. Longfellow. You have no idea how much the laboring men of Cambridge think of him. There is many and many a family that gets a load of coal from Mr. Longfellow, without anybody knowing where it comes from.' . . . The people of Cambridge delighted in Mr. Longfellow's loyalty to the town of his residence and its society. They could not fail to be gratified that he and his family did not seek the society of the neighboring metropolis, or rather usually declined its solicitations, and preferred the simple and familiar ways and old friends of the less pretentious suburban community. Nothing could be more charming than the apparently absolute unconsciousness of distinction which pervaded the intercourse of Mr. Longfellow and his family with Cambridge society."

The title of *Ultima Thule* was a tacit confession that the poet had reached the border of earth, but the last poem in the volume, *The Poet and his Songs*, was a truer confession that the singer must sing when the songs come to him ; and thus from time to time, in the last year of his life, Mr. Longfellow uttered his poems, reading the proof, indeed, of one, *Mad River*, but a few days before his death, the poem appearing in the May number of *The Atlantic*.

As the seventy-fifth anniversary of the poet's birth drew near, there was a spontaneous movement throughout the country looking to the celebration of the day, especially among the school-children. The recitation of his poems by thousands of childish voices was the happiest possible form of honoring him. In his own city of Cambridge all the schools thus remembered him, and numberless schools in the West and South also took the same form of celebration ; while the Historical Society which had its home in his birthplace held a meeting, and its members gave themselves up to pleasant reminiscences of the poet.

He had been confined to the house for several weeks before his last sickness, but in the warm days of early spring had ventured upon his veranda. A neighbor recalls the pretty sight of the gray-haired poet playing with his little grandchild one day in March. It was not until Monday, March 20th, that the fatal illness caused serious alarm; and on Friday, the 24th, the bells tolled his death. His neighbors and the whole community showed their solicitude in those few days. The very children were heard to say, as they passed his gate, "We must tread gently, for Mr. Longfellow is very sick." The message of his death was sent round the world, and probably not a journal in Christendom but had some words, few or many, in regret and honor, upon receipt of the news. On Sunday, March 26, 1882, he was buried from his home, where his family and a few of his nearest friends were gathered. He was laid in Mount Auburn Cemetery, in Cambridge; and that afternoon Appleton Chapel, of Harvard University, was opened for a simple memorial service, thronged by a silent multitude, who listened to the tender discourse of two of the college clergy, to the hymns of the college choir, and to the consolation of the sacred Scriptures.

LONGFELLOW IN HOME LIFE.

BY ALICE M. LONGFELLOW.

MANY people are full of poetry without, perhaps, recognizing it, because they have no power of expression. Some have, unfortunately, full power of expression, with no depth or richness of thought or character behind it. With Mr. Longfellow, there was complete unity and harmony between his life and character and the outward manifestation of this in his poetry. It was not worked out from his brain, but was the blossoming of his inward life.

His nature was thoroughly poetic and rhythmical, full of delicate fancies and thoughts. Even the ordinary details of existence were invested with charm and thoughtfulness. There was really no line of demarcation between his life and his poetry. One blended into the other, and his daily life was poetry in its truest sense. The rhythmical quality showed itself in an exact order and method, running through every detail. This was not the precision of a martinet; but anything out of place distressed him, as did a faulty rhyme or defective metre.

His library was carefully arranged by subjects, and, although no catalogue was ever made, he was never at a loss where to look for any needed volume. His books were deeply beloved and tenderly handled. Beautiful bindings were a great delight, and the leaves were cut with the utmost care and neatness. Letters and bills were kept in the same orderly manner. The latter were paid as soon as rendered, and he always personally attended to those in the neighborhood. An unpaid bill weighed on him like a night-

mare. Letters were answered day by day, as they accumulated, although it became often a weary task. He never
failed, I think, to keep his account books accurately, and he
also used to keep the bank books of the servants in his
employment, and to help them with their accounts.

Consideration and thoughtfulness for others were strong
characteristics with Mr. Longfellow. He, indeed, carried it
too far, and became almost a prey to those he used to call
the " total strangers," whose demands for time and help were
constant. Fortunately he was able to extract much interest
and entertainment from the different types of humanity that
were always coming on one pretext or another, and his
genuine sympathy and quick sense of humor saved the situ-
ation from becoming too wearing. This constant drain was,
however, very great. His unselfishness and courtesy prevented him from showing the weariness of spirit he often
felt, and many valuable hours were taken out of his life by
those with no claim, and no appreciation of what they were
doing.

In addition to the " total strangers " was a long line of
applicants for aid of every kind. " His house was known
to all the vagrant train," and to all he was equally genial
and kind. There was no change of voice or manner in
talking with the humblest member of society ; and I am
inclined to think the friendly chat in Italian with the organ-
grinder and the little old woman peddler, or the discussions
with the old Irish gardener, were quite as full of pleasure as
more important conversations with travelers from Europe.

One habit Mr. Longfellow always kept up. Whenever
he saw in a newspaper any pleasant notice of friends or
acquaintances, a review of a book, or a subject in which
they were interested, he cut it out, and kept the scraps in
an envelope addressed to the person, and mailed them when
several had accumulated.

He was a great foe to procrastination, and believed in
attending to everything without delay. In connection with

this I may say, that when he accepted the invitation of his classmates to deliver a poem at Bowdoin College on the fiftieth anniversary of their graduation, he at once devoted himself to the work, and the poem was finished several months before the time. During these months he was ill with severe neuralgia, and if it had not been for this habit of early preparation the poem would probably never have been written or delivered.

Society and hospitality meant something quite real to Mr. Longfellow. I cannot remember that there were ever any formal or obligatory occasions of entertainment. All who came were made welcome without any special preparation, and without any thought of personal inconvenience.

Mr. Longfellow's knowledge of foreign languages brought to him travelers from every country, — not only literary men, but public men and women of every kind, and, during the stormy days of European politics, great numbers of foreign patriots exiled for their liberal opinions. As one Englishman pleasantly remarked, " There are no ruins in your country to see, Mr. Longfellow, and so we thought we would come to see you."

Mr. Longfellow was a true lover of peace in every way, and held war in absolute abhorrence, as well as the taking of life in any form. He was strongly opposed to capital punishment, and was filled with indignation at the idea of men finding sport in hunting and killing dumb animals. At the same time he was quickly stirred by any story of wrong and oppression, and ready to give a full measure of help and sympathy to any one struggling for freedom and liberty of thought and action.

With political life, as such, Mr. Longfellow was not in full sympathy, in spite of his life-long friendship with Charles Sumner. That is to say, the principles involved deeply interested him, but the methods displeased him. He felt that the intense absorption in one line of thought prevented a full development, and was an enemy to many of the most beautiful and important things in life. He considered that his part was to cast his weight with what seemed to him the best elements in public life, and he never omitted the duty of expressing his opinion by his vote. He always went to the polls the first thing in the morning on election day, and let nothing interfere with this. He used to say laughingly that he still belonged to the Federalists.

Mr. Longfellow came to Cambridge to live in 1837, when he was thirty years old. He was at that time professor of literature in Harvard College, and occupied two rooms in the old house then owned by the widow Craigie, formerly Washington's Headquarters. In this same old house he passed the remainder of his life, being absent only one year in foreign travel. Home had great attractions for him. He cared more for the quiet and repose, the companionship of his friends and books, than for the fatigues and adventures of new scenes. Many of the friends of his youth were the friends of old age, and to them his house was always open with a warm welcome.

Mr. Longfellow was always full of reserve, and never talked much about himself or his work, even to his family. Sometimes a volume would appear in print, without his having mentioned its preparation. In spite of his general interest in people, only a few came really close to his life. With these he was always glad to go over the early days passed together, and to consult with them about literary work.

The lines descriptive of the Student in the Wayside Inn might apply to Mr. Longfellow as well : —

> " A youth was there, of quiet ways,
> A Student of old books and days,
> To whom all tongues and lands were known,
> And yet a lover of his own ;
> With many a social virtue graced,
> And yet a friend of solitude ;
> A man of such a genial mood
> The heart of all things he embraced,
> And yet of such fastidious taste,
> He never found the best too good."

Map of The Basin of Minas and the Old Acadian Land.

PARRSBORO

MINAS CHANNEL

Cape Blomidon

BASIN OF MINAS

GRAND PRÉ

KENTVILLE

Gaspereau R.

WINDSOR

PRINCE EDWARD ISLAND

CAPE BRETON ISLAND

Beau Sejour

Basin of Minas

NOVA SCOTIA

Bay of Fundy

Port Royal

GRAND PRÉ

Louisburg Cape Breton

ATLANTIC OCEAN

THE MATTHEWS-NORTHRUP CO. BUFFALO, N.Y.

EVANGELINE: A TALE OF ACADIE.

THE country now known as Nova Scotia, and called formerly Acadie by the French, was in the hands of the French and English by turns until the year 1713, when, by the Peace of Utrecht, it was ceded by France to Great Britain, and has ever since remained in the possession of the English. But in 1713 the inhabitants of the peninsula were mostly French farmers and fishermen, living about Minas Basin and on Annapolis River, and the English government exercised only a nominal control over them. It was not till 1749 that the English themselves began to make settlements in the country, and that year they laid the foundations of the town of Halifax. A jealousy soon sprang up between the English and French settlers, which was deepened by the great conflict which was impending between the two mother countries ; for the treaty of peace at Aix-la-Chapelle in 1748, which confirmed the English title to Nova Scotia, was scarcely more than a truce between the two powers which had been struggling for ascendency during the beginning of the century. The French engaged in a long controversy with the English respecting the boundaries of Acadie, which had been defined by the treaties in somewhat general terms, and intrigues were carried on with the Indians, who were generally in sympathy with the French, for the annoyance of the English settlers. The Acadians were allied to the French by blood and by religion, but they claimed to have the rights of neutrals, and that these rights had been granted to them by previous English officers of the crown. The one point of special dispute was the oath of allegiance demanded of the Acadians by the English. This they refused to take, except in a form modified to excuse them from bearing arms against the French. The demand was repeatedly made, and evaded with constant ingenuity and persistency. Most of the Acadians were probably simple-minded and peaceful people, who desired only to live undisturbed upon their farms; but there were some restless spirits, especially among the young men, who compromised the reputation of the community, and all were very much under the influence of their priests, some of whom made no secret of their bitter hostility to the English, and of their determination to use every means to be rid of them.

As the English interests grew and the critical relations between the two countries approached open warfare, the question of how to deal with the Acadian problem became the commanding one of the colony. There were some who coveted the rich farms of the Acadians; there were some who were inspired by religious hatred; but the prevailing spirit was one of fear for themselves from the near presence of a community which, calling itself neutral, might at any time offer a convenient ground for hostile attack. Yet to require these people to withdraw to Canada or Louisburg would be to strengthen the hands of the French, and make these neutrals determined enemies. The colony finally resolved, without consulting the home government, to remove the Acadians to other parts of North America, distributing them through the colonies in such a way as to preclude any concert amongst the scattered families by which they should return to Acadia. To do this required quick and secret preparations. There were at the service of the English governor a number of New England troops, brought thither for the capture of the forts lying in the debatable land about the head of the Bay of Fundy. These were under the command of Lieutenant-Colonel John Winslow, of Massachu-

setts, a great-grandson of Governor Edward Winslow, of
Plymouth, and to this gentleman and Captain Alexander
Murray was intrusted the task of removal. They were instructed to use stratagem, if possible, to bring together the
various families, but to prevent any from escaping to the
woods. On the 2d of September, 1755, Winslow issued a
written order, addressed to the inhabitants of Grand-Pré,
Minas, River Canard, etc., "as well ancient as young men
and lads," — a proclamation summoning all the males to
attend him in the church at Grand-Pré on the 5th instant,
to hear a communication which the governor had sent. As
there had been negotiations respecting the oath of allegiance,
and much discussion as to the withdrawal of the Acadians
from the country, though none as to their removal and dis-
persal, it was understood that this was an important meeting, and upon the day named four hundred and eighteen
men and boys assembled in the church. Winslow, attended
by his officers and men, caused a guard to be placed round
the church, and then announced to the people his majesty's
decision that they were to be removed with their families
out of the country. The church became at once a guard-
house, and all the prisoners were under strict surveillance.
At the same time similar plans had been carried out at Pisi-
quid under Captain Murray, and less successfully at Chig-
necto. Meanwhile there were whispers of a rising among
the prisoners, and although the transports which had been
ordered from Boston had not yet arrived, it was determined
to make use of the vessels which had conveyed the troops,
and remove the men to these for safer keeping. This was
done on the 10th of September, and the men remained on
the vessels in the harbor until the arrival of the transports,
when these were made use of, and about three thousand
souls sent out of the country to North Carolina, Virginia,
Maryland, Pennsylvania, New York, Connecticut, and Massachusetts. In the haste and confusion of sending them off,
— a haste which was increased by the anxiety of the offi-

cers to be rid of the distasteful business, and a confusion
which was greater from the difference of tongues, — many
families were separated, and some at least never came together again.

The story of Evangeline is the story of such a separation.
The removal of the Acadians was a blot upon the government of Nova Scotia and upon that of Great Britain, which
never disowned the deed, although it was probably done
without direct permission or command from England.   It
proved to be unnecessary, but it must also be remembered
that to many men at that time the English power seemed
trembling before France, and that the colony at Halifax
regarded the act as one of self-preservation.

The authorities for an historical inquiry into this subject
are best seen in a volume published by the government of
Nova Scotia at Halifax in 1869, entitled *Selections from
the Public Documents of the Province of Nova Scotia*,
edited by Thomas B. Akins, D. C. L., Commissioner of
Public Records ; and in a manuscript journal kept by Colonel Winslow, now in the cabinet of the Massachusetts Historical Society in Boston.   At the State House in Boston
are two volumes of records, entitled *French Neutrals*, which
contain voluminous papers relating to the treatment of the
Acadians who were sent to Massachusetts.   Probably the
work used by the poet in writing *Evangeline* was *An Historical and Statistical Account of Nova Scotia*, by Thomas
C. Haliburton, who is best known as the author of *The Clock-
Maker, or The Sayings and Doings of Samuel Slick of
Slickville*, a book which, written apparently to prick the
Nova Scotians into more enterprise, was for a long while the
chief representative of Yankee smartness.   Judge Haliburt-
ton's history was published in 1829.   A later history, which
takes advantage more freely of historical documents, is *A
History of Nova Scotia, or Acadie*, by Beamish Murdock,
Esq., Q. C., Halifax, 1866.   Still more recent is a smaller,
well-written work, entitled *The History of Acadia from its*

First Discovery to its Surrender to England by the Treaty of Paris, by James Hannay, St. John, N. B., 1879. W. J. Anderson published a paper in the *Transactions* of the Literary and Historical Society of Quebec. New Series, part 7. 1870, entitled *Evangeline and the Archives of Nova Scotia*, in which he examines the poem by the light of the volume of Nova Scotia *Archives*, edited by T. B. Akins. The sketches of travellers in Nova Scotia, as *Acadia, or a Month among the Blue Noses*, by F. S. Cozzens, and *Baddeck*, by C. D. Warner, give the present appearance of the country and inhabitants.

HISTORY OF THE POEM.

The origin of the tale brings out one of those interesting incidents of the relations of authors toward each other which happily are not uncommon. In Hawthorne's *American Note-Books*, under date of October 24, 1838, occurs this paragraph: " H. L. C—— heard from a French Canadian a story of a young couple in Acadie. On their marriage day, all the men of the province were summoned to assemble in the church to hear a proclamation. When assembled, they were all seized and shipped off to be distributed through New England, among them the new bridegroom. His bride set off in search of him, wandered about New England all her life-time, and at last, when she was old, she found her bridegroom on his death-bed. The shock was so great that it killed her likewise."

It may have been the same H. L. C. who dined with Hawthorne at Mr. Longfellow's one day, and told the poet that he had been trying to persuade Hawthorne to write a story on this theme. Hawthorne said he could not see in it the material for a tale, but Longfellow at once caught at it as the suggestion for a poem. "Give it to me." he said, " and promise that you will not write about it until I have written the poem." Hawthorne readily consented, and when *Evangeline* appeared was as quick to give expression

to his admiration as the poet had been in reviewing
Twice-Told Tales. He wrote to Longfellow and sent him
a copy of a Salem newspaper in which he had noticed
Evangeline. Longfellow replied : —

MY DEAR HAWTHORNE, — I have been waiting and waiting
in the hope of seeing you in Cambridge. . . . I have been medi-
tating upon your letter, and pondering with friendly admiration
your review of *Evangeline*, in connection with the subject of
which, that is to say, the Acadians, a literary project arises in
my mind for you to execute. Perhaps I can pay you back in
part your own generous gift, by giving you a theme for story
in return for a theme for song. It is neither more nor less than
the history of the Acadians *after* their expulsion as well as before.
Felton has been making some researches in the state archives,
and offers to resign the documents into your hands.

Pray come and see me about it without delay. Come so as to
pass a night with us, if possible, this week, if not a day and
night. Ever sincerely yours,   HENRY W. LONGFELLOW.

The poet never visited the scenes of his poem, though
travellers have testified to the accuracy of the portraiture.
"I have never been in Nova Scotia," he wrote to a friend.
"As far as I remember, the authorities I mostly relied on in
writing *Evangeline* were the Abbé Raynal and Mr. Haliburton : the first for the pastoral, simple life of the Acadians ; the second for the history of their banishment."
He gave to a Philadelphia journalist a reminiscence of his
first thought of the material which forms the conclusion of
the poem. "I was passing down Spruce Street one day
toward my hotel, after a walk, when my attention was attracted to a large building with beautiful trees about it,
inside of a high inclosure. I walked along until I came to
the great gate, and then stepped inside, and looked carefully over the place. The charming picture of lawn, flower-
beds, and shade which it presented made an impression
which has never left me, and when I came to write *Evangeline* I placed the final scene, the meeting between Evangeline

and Gabriel and the death, at the poor-house, and the burial in an old Catholic grave-yard not far away, which I found by chance in another of my walks."

The poem made its way at once into the hearts of people. Faed, an English artist, painted a picture of Evangeline, taken from the face of a Manchester working-girl, which his brother engraved, and the picture became a great favorite on both continents.

THE MEASURE.

The measure of *Evangeline* is what is commonly known as English dactylic hexameter. The hexameter is the measure used by Homer in the *Iliad* and the *Odyssey*, and by Virgil in the *Æneid*, but the difference between the English language and the Latin or Greek is so great, especially when we consider that in English poetry every word must be accented according to its customary pronunciation, while in scanning Greek and Latin verse accent follows the quantity of the vowels, that in applying this term of hexameter to *Evangeline* it must not be supposed by the reader that he is getting the effect of Greek hexameters. It is the Greek hexameter translated into English use, and some have maintained that the verse of the *Iliad* is better represented in the English by the trochaic measure of fifteen syllables, of which an excellent illustration is in Tennyson's *Locksley Hall;* others have compared the Greek hexameter to the ballad metre of fourteen syllables, used notably by Chapman in his translation of Homer's *Iliad.* The measure adopted by Mr. Longfellow has never become very popular in English poetry, but has repeatedly been attempted by other poets. The reader will find the subject of hexameters discussed by Matthew Arnold in his lectures *On Translating Homer;* by James Spedding in *English Hexameters,* in his recent volume, *Reviews and Discussions, Literary. Political and Historical, not relating to Bacon;* and by John Stuart Blackie in *Remarks on Eng-*

lish Hexameters, contained in his volume *Horæ Hellenicæ*. The publication of *Evangeline* had much to do with the revival of the use of the hexameter in English poetry, notably by Arthur Hugh Clough, who employed it with great skill in his pastoral poem of the *Bothie of Tober-na-Vuolich*. In a letter to Ralph Waldo Emerson, Clough writes, " Will you convey to Mr. Longfellow the fact that it was a reading of his *Evangeline* aloud to my mother and sister, which, coming after a reperusal of the Iliad, occasioned this outbreak of hexameters ? "

The measure lends itself easily to the lingering melancholy which marks the greater part of the poem, and the poet's fine sense of harmony between subject and form is rarely better shown than in this poem. The fall of the verse at the end of the line and the sharp recovery at the beginning of the next will be snares to the reader, who must beware of a jerking style of delivery. The voice naturally seeks a rest in the middle of the line, and this rest, or cæsural pause, should be carefully regarded : a little practice will enable one to acquire that habit of reading the hexameter, which we may liken, roughly, to the climbing of a hill, resting a moment on the summit, and then descending the other side. The charm in reading *Evangeline* aloud, after a clear understanding of the sense, which is the essential in all good reading, is found in this gentle labor of the former half of the line, and gentle acceleration of the latter half.

EVANGELINE.

PRELUDE.

THIS is the forest primeval. The murmuring pines
  and the hemlocks,
Bearded with moss, and in garments green, indistinct
  in the twilight,
Stand like Druids of eld, with voices sad and prophetic,

1. A primeval forest is, strictly speaking, one which has never
been disturbed by the axe. Dr. Oliver Wendell Holmes, remark-
ing on this opening of the poem, says : " From the first line of
the poem, from its first words, we read as we would float down
a broad and placid river, murmuring softly against its banks,
heaven over it, and the glory of the unspoiled wilderness all
around.

"' This is the forest primeval.'

The words are already as familiar as

Μῆνιν ἄειδε θεά,

or

Arma virumque cano.

The hexameter has been often criticised, but I do not believe
any other measure could have told that lovely story with such
effect as we feel when carried along the tranquil current of
these brimming, slow-moving, soul-satisfying lines. Imagine
for one moment a story like this minced into octosyllabics. The
poet knows better than his critics the length of step which best
fits his muse."

3. *Druids* were priests of the Celtic inhabitants of ancient
Gaul and Britain. The name was probably of Celtic origin, but
its form may have been determined by the Greek word *drūs*, an
oak, since their places of worship were consecrated groves of
oak. Perhaps the choice of the image was governed by the
analogy of a religion and tribe that were to disappear before a
stronger power.

Stand like harpers hoar, with beards that rest on their
    bosoms.
Loud from its rocky caverns, the deep-voiced neigh-
    boring ocean   5
Speaks, and in accents disconsolate answers the wail
    of the forest.

  This is the forest primeval; but where are the
    hearts that beneath it
Leaped like the roe, when he hears in the woodland
    the voice of the huntsman?
Where is the thatch-roofed village, the home of Aca-
    dian farmers, —
Men whose lives glided on like rivers that water the
    woodlands,   10
Darkened by shadows of earth, but reflecting an image
    of heaven?
Waste are those pleasant farms, and the farmers for-
    ever departed!
Scattered like dust and leaves, when the mighty blasts
    of October
Seize them, and whirl them aloft, and sprinkle them
    far o'er the ocean.
Naught but tradition remains of the beautiful village
    of Grand-Pré.   15

  Ye who believe in affection that hopes, and endures,
    and is patient,

4. A poetical description of an ancient harper will be found
in the *Introduction* to the *Lay of the Last Minstrel*, by Sir Walter
Scott.

  8. Observe how the tragedy of the story is anticipated by this
picture of the startled roe.

Ye who believe in the beauty and strength of woman's
     devotion,
List to the mournful tradition still sung by the pines
     of the forest;
List to a Tale of Love in Acadie, home of the happy

PART THE FIRST.

I.

In the Acadian land, on the shores of the Basin of
     Minas,   20
Distant, secluded, still, the little village of Grand-Pré
Lay in the fruitful valley. Vast meadows stretched
     to the eastward,
Giving the village its name, and pasture to flocks
     without number.
Dikes, that the hands of the farmers had raised with
     labor incessant,

19. In the earliest records *Acadie* is called Cadie ; it afterwards was called Arcadia, Accadia, or L'Acadie. The name is
probably a French adaptation of a word common among the
Micmac Indians living there, signifying place or region, and used
as an affix to other words as indicating the place where various
things, as cranberries, eels, seals, were found in abundance. The
French turned this Indian term into Cadie or Acadie ; the English into Quoddy, in which form it remains when applied to the
Quoddy Indians, to Quoddy Head, the last point of the United
States next to Acadia, and in the compound Passamaquoddy, or
Pollock-Ground.

21. Compare, for effect, the first line of Goldsmith's *The
Traveller*. Grand-Pré will be found on the map as part of the
township of Horton.

24. The people of Acadia are mainly the descendants of the
colonists who were brought out to La Have and Port Royal by
Isaac de Razilly and Charnisay between the years 1633 and 1638.

Shut out the turbulent tides; but at stated seasons the
    flood-gates   25
Opened and welcomed the sea to wander at will o'er
    the meadows.
West and south there were fields of flax, and orchards
    and cornfields
Spreading afar and unfenced o'er the plain; and away
    to the northward
Blomidon rose, and the forests old, and aloft on the
    mountains
Sea-fogs pitched their tents, and mists from the mighty
    Atlantic   30
Looked on the happy valley, but ne'er from their sta-
    tion descended.
There, in the midst of its farms, reposed the Acadian
    village.
Strongly built were the houses, with frames of oak and
    of hemlock,
Such as the peasants of Normandy built in the reign
    of the Henries.

These colonists came from Rochelle, Saintonge, and Poitou, so
that they were drawn from a very limited area on the west coast
of France, covered by the modern departments of Vendée and
Charente Inférieure. This circumstance had some influence on
their mode of settling the lands of Acadia, for they came from a
country of marshes, where the sea was kept out by artificial
dikes, and they found in Acadia similar marshes, which they dealt
with in the same way that they had been accustomed to practise
in France. Hannay's *History of Acadia*, pp. 282, 283. An excellent account of dikes and the flooding of lowlands, as practised
in Holland, may be found in *A Farmer's Vacation*, by George E.
Waring, Jr.

   29. *Blomidon* is a mountainous headland of red sandstone, sur-
mounted by a perpendicular wall of basaltic trap, the whole about
four hundred feet in height, at the entrance of the Basin of
Minas.

Thatched were the roofs, with dormer-windows; and
 gables projecting   35
Over the basement below protected and shaded the
 doorway.
There in the tranquil evenings of summer, when
 brightly the sunset
Lighted the village street, and gilded the vanes on the
 chimneys,
Matrons and maidens sat in snow-white caps and in
 kirtles
Scarlet and blue and green, with distaffs spinning the
 golden   40
Flax for the gossiping looms, whose noisy shuttles
 within doors
Mingled their sound with the whir of the wheels and
 the songs of the maidens.
Solemnly down the street came the parish priest, and
 the children
Paused in their play to kiss the hand he extended to
 bless them.
Reverend walked he among them; and up rose matrons and maidens,   45
Hailing his slow approach with words of affectionate
 welcome.
Then came the laborers home from the field, and serenely the sun sank

36. The characteristics of a Normandy village may be further
learned by reference to a pleasant little sketch-book, published
a few years since, called *Normandy Picturesque*, by Henry Black-
burn, and to *Through Normandy*, by Katharine S. Macquoid.

39. The term *kirtle* was sometimes applied to the jacket only,
sometimes to the train or upper petticoat attached to it. A full
kirtle was always both; a half kirtle was a term applied to
either. A man's jacket was sometimes called a kirtle; here the
reference is apparently to the full kirtle worn by women.

Down to his rest, and twilight prevailed.   Anon from
    the belfry
Softly the Angelus sounded, and over the roofs of the
    village
Columns of pale blue smoke, like clouds of incense
    ascending,   50
Rose from a hundred hearths, the homes of peace and
    contentment.
Thus dwelt together in love these simple Acadian
    farmers, —
Dwelt in the love of God and of man.   Alike were
    they free from
Fear, that reigns with the tyrant, and envy, the vice
    of republics.
Neither locks had they to their doors, nor bars to their
    windows ;   55
But their dwellings were open as day and the hearts
    of the owners ;
There the richest was poor and the poorest lived in
    abundance.

    Somewhat apart from the village, and nearer the
    Basin of Minas,
Benedict Bellefontaine, the wealthiest farmer of
    Grand-Pré,
Dwelt on his goodly acres; and with him, directing
    his household,   60
Gentle Evangeline lived, his child, and the pride of
    the village.

49. *Angelus Domini* is the full name given to the bell which, at
morning, noon, and night, called the people to prayer, in com-
memoration of the visit of the angel of the Lord to the Virgin
Mary.   It was introduced into France in its modern form in the
sixteenth century.

Stalworth and stately in form was the man of seventy
    winters ;

Hearty and hale was he, an oak that is covered with
    snow-flakes ;

White as the snow were his locks, and his cheeks as
    brown as the oak-leaves.

Fair was she to behold, that maiden of seventeen sum-
    mers ;   65

Black were her eyes as the berry that grows on the
    thorn by the wayside,

Black, yet how softly they gleamed beneath the brown
    shade of her tresses !

Sweet was her breath as the breath of kine that feed
    in the meadows.

When in the harvest heat she bore to the reapers at
    noontide

Flagons of home-brewed ale, ah ! fair in sooth was the
    maiden.   70

Fairer was she when, on Sunday morn, while the bell
    from its turret

Sprinkled with holy sounds the air, as the priest with
    his hyssop

Sprinkles the congregation, and scatters blessings upon
    them,

Down the long street she passed, with her chaplet of
    beads and her missal,

Wearing her Norman cap and her kirtle of blue, and
    the ear-rings   75

Brought in the olden time from France, and since, as
    an heirloom,

Handed down from mother to child, through long gen-
    erations.

But a celestial brightness — a more ethereal beauty —

Shone on her face and encircled her form, when, after
    confession,

Homeward serenely she walked with God's benediction upon her.   80

When she had passed, it seemed like the ceasing of exquisite music.)

Firmly builded with rafters of oak, the house of the farmer

Stood on the side of a hill commanding the sea: and a shady

Sycamore grew by the door, with a woodbine wreathing around it.

Rudely carved was the porch, with seats beneath ; and a footpath   85

Led through an orchard wide, and disappeared in the meadow.

Under the sycamore-tree were hives overhung by a penthouse,

Such as the traveller sees in regions remote by the roadside,

Built o'er a box for the poor, or the blessed image of Mary.

Farther down, on the slope of the hill, was the well with its moss-grown   90

Bucket, fastened with iron, and near it a trough for the horses.

Shielding the house from storms, on the north, were the barns and the farm-yard ;

There stood the broad-wheeled wains and the antique ploughs and the harrows ;

There were the folds for the sheep ; and there, in his feathered seraglio,

---

93. The accent is on the first syllable of *antique*, where it remains in the form *antic*, which once had the same general meaning.

Strutted the lordly turkey, and crowed the cock, with the selfsame   95

Voice that in ages of old had startled the penitent Peter.

Bursting with hay were the barns, themselves a village.   In each one

Far o'er the gable projected a roof of thatch ; and a staircase,

Under the sheltering eaves, led up to the odorous corn-loft.

There too the dove-cot stood, with its meek and innocent inmates   100

Murmuring ever of love ; while above in the variant breezes

Numberless noisy weathercocks rattled and sang of mutation.

Thus, at peace with God and the world, the farmer of Grand-Pré

Lived on his sunny farm, and Evangeline governed his household.

Many a youth, as he knelt in the church and opened his missal,   105

Fixed his eyes upon her as the saint of his deepest devotion ;

99. *Odorous.*   The accent here, as well as in line 403, is upon the first syllable, where it is commonly placed ; but Milton, who of all poets had the most refined ear, writes

> " So from the root
> Springs lighter the green stalk, from thence the leaves
> More airy, last the bright consummate flower
> Spirits odorous breathes."
> *Par Lost*, Book V., lines 479–482.

But he also uses the more familiar accent in other passages, as, " An amber scent of ódorous perfume," in *Sumson Agonistes*, line 720.

Happy was he who might touch her hand or the hem
    of her garment!
Many a suitor came to her door, by the darkness be·
    friended,
And, as he knocked and waited to hear the sound of
    her footsteps,
Knew not which beat the louder, his heart or the
    knocker of iron;   110
Or, at the joyous feast of the Patron Saint of the vil-
    lage,
Bolder grew, and pressed her hand in the dance as he
    whispered
Hurried words of love, that seemed a part of the
    music.
But among all who came young Gabriel only was
    welcome;
Gabriel Lajeunesse, the son of Basil the black-
    smith,   115
Who was a mighty man in the village, and honored
    of all men;
For since the birth of time, throughout all ages and
    nations,
Has the craft of the smith been held in repute by the
    people.
Basil was Benedict's friend. Their children from
    earliest childhood
Grew up together as brother and sister: and Father
    Felician,   120
Priest and pedagogue both in the village, had taught
    them their letters
Out of the selfsame book, with the hymns of the
    church and the plain-song.

122. The *plain-song* is a monotonic recitative of the collects.

But when the hymn was sung, and the daily lesson
    completed,
Swiftly they hurried away to the forge of Basil the
    blacksmith.
There at the door they stood, with wondering eyes to
    behold him   125
Take in his leathern lap the hoof of the horse as a
    plaything,
Nailing the shoe in its place; while near him the tire
    of the cart-wheel
Lay like a fiery snake, coiled round in a circle of
    cinders.
Oft on autumnal eves, when without in the gathering
    darkness
Bursting with light seemed the smithy, through every
    cranny and crevice,   130
Warm by the forge within they watched the laboring
    bellows,
And as its panting ceased, and the sparks expired in
    the ashes,
Merrily laughed, and said they were nuns going into
    the chapel.
Oft on sledges in winter, as swift as the swoop of the
    eagle,
Down the hillside bounding, they glided away o'er the
    meadow.   135
Oft in the barns they climbed to the populous nests
    on the rafters,
Seeking with eager eyes that wondrous stone, which
    the swallow
Brings from the shore of the sea to restore the sight
    of its fledglings;

133. The French have another saying similar to this, that they
were guests going in to the wedding.

Lucky was he who found that stone in the nest of the
 swallow!
Thus passed a few swift years, and they no longer
 were children.   140
He was a valiant youth, and his face, like the face of
 the morning,
Gladdened the earth with its light, and ripened
 thought into action.
She was a woman now, with the heart and hopes of a
 woman.
" Sunshine of Saint Eulalie " was she called ; for that
 was the sunshine
Which, as the farmers believed, would load their
 orchards with apples ;   145
She too would bring to her husband's house delight
 and abundance,
Filling it with love and the ruddy faces of children.

II.

Now had the season returned, when the nights grow
 colder and longer,
And the retreating sun the sign of the Scorpion en-
 ters.

139. In Pluquet's *Contes Populaires* we are told that if one of
a swallow's young is blind the mother bird seeks on the shore of
the ocean a little stone, with which she restores its sight ; and
he adds, " He who is fortunate enough to find that stone in a
swallow's nest holds a wonderful remedy."   Pluquet's book
treats of Norman superstitions and popular traits.

144. Pluquet also gives this proverbial saying : —

> " Si le soleil rit le jour Sainte-Eulalie,
> Il y aura pommes et cidre à folie."

(If the sun smiles on Saint Eulalie's day, there will be plenty
of apples, and cider enough.)

Saint Eulalie's day is the 12th of February.

Birds of passage sailed through the leaden air, from
    the ice-bound,   150
Desolate northern bays to the shores of tropical is-
    lands.
Harvests were gathered in ; and wild with the winds
    of September
Wrestled the trees of the forest, as Jacob of old with
    the angel.
All the signs foretold a winter long and inclement.
Bees, with prophetic instinct of want, had hoarded
    their honey   155
Till the hives overflowed ; and the Indian hunters as-
    serted
Cold would the winter be, for thick was the fur of the
    foxes.
Such was the advent of autumn. Then followed that
    beautiful season,
Called by the pious Acadian peasants the Summer of
    All-Saints !
Filled was the air with a dreamy and magical light ;
    and the landscape   160
Lay as if new-created in all the freshness of child-
    hood.
Peace seemed to reign upon earth, and the restless
    heart of the ocean
Was for a moment consoled. All sounds were in
    harmony blended.
Voices of children at play, the crowing of cocks in the
    farm-yards,

159. The Summer of All-Saints is our Indian Summer, All-
Saints Day being November 1st. The French also give this season the name of Saint Martin's Summer, Saint Martin's Day
being November 11th.

Whir of wings in the drowsy air, and the cooing of
    pigeons,   165
All were subdued and low as the murmurs of love,
    and the great sun
Looked with the eye of love through the golden va
    pors around him ;
While arrayed in its robes of russet and scarlet and
    yellow,
Bright with the sheen of the dew, each glittering tree
    of the forest
Flashed like the plane-tree the Persian adorned with
    mantles and jewels.   170

   Now recommenced the region of rest and affection
    and stillness.
Day with its burden and heat had departed, and twi-
    light descending
Brought back the evening star to the sky, and the
    herds to the homestead.
Pawing the ground they came, and resting their necks
    on each other,
And with their nostrils distended inhaling the fresh-
    ness of evening.   175
Foremost, bearing the bell, Evangeline's beautiful
    heifer,
Proud of her snow-white hide, and the ribbon that
    waved from her collar.
Quietly paced and slow, as if conscious of human
    affection.

   170. Herodotus, in his account of Xerxes' expedition against
Greece, tells of a beautiful plane-tree which Xerxes found, and
was so enamored with that he dressed it as one might a woman,
and placed it under the care of a guardsman (vii. 31). Another
writer, Ælian, improving on this, says he adorned it with a necklace and bracelets.

Then came the shepherd back with his bleating flocks
from the seaside,
Where was their favorite pasture. Behind them followed the watch-dog,   180
Patient, full of importance, and grand in the pride of
his instinct,
Walking from side to side with a lordly air, and
superbly
Waving his bushy tail, and urging forward the strag-
glers;
Regent of flocks was he when the shepherd slept;
their protector,
When from the forest at night, through the starry
silence, the wolves howled.   185
Late, with the rising moon, returned the wains from
the marshes,
Laden with briny hay, that filled the air with its odor.
Cheerily neighed the steeds, with dew on their manes
and their fetlocks,
While aloft on their shoulders the wooden and ponderous saddles,
Painted with brilliant dyes, and adorned with tassels
of crimson,   190
Nodded in bright array, like hollyhocks heavy with
blossoms.
Patiently stood the cows meanwhile, and yielded their
udders
Unto the milkmaid's hand; whilst loud and in regular
cadence

---

193. There is a charming milkmaid's song in Tennyson's drama
of *Queen Mary*, Act III., Scene 5, where the streaming of the
milk into the sounding pails is caught in the tinkling *k's* of such
lines as
"And you came and kissed me milking the cow."

Into the sounding pails the foaming streamlets de-
    scended.
Lowing of cattle and peals of laughter were heard in
    the farm-yard,   195
Echoed back by the barns. Anon they sank into
    stillness ;
Heavily closed, with a jarring sound, the valves of the
    barn-doors,
Rattled the wooden bars, and all for a season was silent.

In-doors, warm by the wide-mouthed fireplace, idly
    the farmer
Sat in his elbow-chair, and watched how the flames
    and the smoke-wreaths   200
Struggled together like foes in a burning city. Be-
    hind him,
Nodding and mocking along the wall with gestures
    fantastic,
Darted his own huge shadow, and vanished away into
    darkness.
Faces, clumsily carved in oak, on the back of his arm-
    chair
Laughed in the flickering light, and the pewter plates
    on the dresser   205
Caught and reflected the flame, as shields of armies
    the sunshine.
Fragments of song the old man sang, and carols of
    Christmas,
Such as at home, in the olden time, his fathers before
    him
Sang in their Norman orchards and bright Burgundian
    vineyards.
Close at her father's side was the gentle Evangeline
    seated,   210

Spinning flax for the loom that stood in the corner
    behind her.
Silent awhile were its treadles, at rest was its diligent
    shuttle,
While the monotonous drone of the wheel, like the
    drone of a bagpipe,
Followed the old man's song, and united the fragments
    together.
As in a church, when the chant of the choir at inter-
    vals ceases,   215
Footfalls are heard in the aisles, or words of the priest
    at the altar,
So, in each pause of the song, with measured motion
    the clock clicked.

    Thus as they sat, there were footsteps heard, and,
    suddenly lifted,
Sounded the wooden latch, and the door swung back
    on its hinges.
Benedict knew by the hob-nailed shoes it was Basil
    the blacksmith,   220
And by her beating heart Evangeline knew who was
    with him.
" Welcome ! " the farmer exclaimed, as their footsteps
    paused on the threshold,
" Welcome, Basil, my friend ! Come, take thy place
    on the settle
Close by the chimney-side, which is always empty
    without thee ;
Take from the shelf overhead thy pipe and the box of
    tobacco ;   225
Never so much thyself art thou as when, through the
    curling
Smoke of the pipe or the forge, thy friendly and jovial
    face gleams

Round and red as the harvest moon through the mist
of the marshes."
Then, with a smile of content, thus answered Basil the
blacksmith,
Taking with easy air the accustomed seat by the fire
side : —   230
"Benedict Bellefontaine, thou hast ever thy jest and
thy ballad !
Ever in cheerfullest mood art thou, when others are
filled with
Gloomy forebodings of ill, and see only ruin before
them.
Happy art thou, as if every day thou hadst picked up
a horseshoe."
Pausing a moment, to take the pipe that Evangeline
brought him,   235
And with a coal from the embers had lighted, he
slowly continued : —
" Four days now are passed since the English ships
at their anchors
Ride in the Gaspereau's mouth, with their cannon
pointed against us.
What their design may be is unknown ; but all are
commanded
On the morrow to meet in the church, where his
Majesty's mandate   240
Will be proclaimed as law in the land.   Alas ! in the
mean time
Many surmises of evil alarm the hearts of the peo-
ple."
Then made answer the farmer : — " Perhaps some
friendlier purpose

239. The text of Colonel Winslow's proclamation will be found
in *Haliburton*, i. 175.

Brings these ships to our shores.   Perhaps the har-
  vests in England
By untimely rains or untimelier heat have been
  blighted,   245
And from our bursting barns they would feed their
  cattle and children."
" Not so thinketh the folk in the village," said warmly
  the blacksmith,
Shaking his head as in doubt; then, heaving a sigh,
  he continued : —
" Louisburg is not forgotten, nor Beau Séjour, nor
  Port Royal.
Many already have fled to the forest, and lurk on its
  outskirts,   250
Waiting with anxious hearts the dubious fate of to-
  morrow.
Arms have been taken from us, and warlike weapons
  of all kinds;
Nothing is left but the blacksmith's sledge and the
  scythe of the mower."
Then with a pleasant smile made answer the jovial
  farmer : —

249. Louisburg, on Cape Breton, was built by the French as a
military and naval station early in the eighteenth century, but
was taken by an expedition from Massachusetts under General
Pepperell in 1745.   It was restored by England to France in the
treaty of Aix-la-Chapelle, and recaptured by the English in
1757.   Beau Séjour was a French fort upon the neck of land
connecting Acadia with the mainland which had just been cap-
tured by Winslow's forces.   Port Royal, afterwards called Annapolis Royal, at the outlet of Annapolis River into the Bay of
Fundy, had been disputed ground, being occupied alternately by
French and English, but in 1710 was attacked by an expedition
from New England, and after that held by the English government and made a fortified place.

" Safer are we unarmed, in the midst of our flocks
　　and our cornfields,　　　　　　　　　　　255
Safer within these peaceful dikes besieged by the ocean,
Than our fathers in forts, besieged by the enemy's
　　cannon.
Fear no evil, my friend, and to-night may no shadow
　　of sorrow
Fall on this house and hearth ; for this is the night
　　of the contract.
Built are the house and the barn.　The merry lads of
　　the village　　　　　　　　　　　　　260
Strongly have built them and well ; and, breaking the
　　glebe round about them,
Filled the barn with hay, and the house with food for
　　a twelvemonth.
René Leblanc will be here anon, with his papers and
　　inkhorn.
Shall we not then be glad, and rejoice in the joy of
　　our children ? "
As apart by the window she stood, with her hand in
　　her lover's,　　　　　　　　　　　　265
Blushing Evangeline heard the words that her father
　　had spoken,
And, as they died on his lips, the worthy notary en-
　　tered.

III.

Bent like a laboring oar, that toils in the surf of
　　the ocean,

267.　A *notary* is an officer authorized to attest contracts or
writings of any kind.　His authority varies in different countries ; in France he is the necessary maker of all contracts where
the subject-matter exceeds 150 francs, and his instruments,
which are preserved and registered by himself, are the origi-
nals, the parties preserving only copies.

Bent, but not broken, by age was the form of the notary public ;

Shocks of yellow hair, like the silken floss of the
maize, hung   27C

Over his shoulders ; his forehead was high ; and
glasses with horn bows

Sat astride on his nose, with a look of wisdom supernal

Father of twenty children was he, and more than a
hundred

Children's children rode on his knee, and heard his
great watch tick.

Four long years in the times of the war had he languished a captive,   275

Suffering much in an old French fort as the friend of
the English.

Now, though warier grown, without all guile or sus-
picion,

Ripe in wisdom was he, but patient, and simple, and
childlike.

He was beloved by all, and most of all by the children ;

For he told them tales of the Loup-garou in the forest,   280

275. King George's War, which broke out in 1744 in Cape
Breton, in an attack by the French upon an English garrison.
and closed with the peace of Aix-la-Chapelle in 1748 ; or, the
reference may possibly be to Queen Anne's war, 1702-1713
when the French aided the Indians in their warfare with the colonists.

280. The *Loup-garou*, or were-wolf, is, according to an old superstition especially prevalent in France, a man with power to
turn himself into a wolf, which he does that he may devour children. In later times the superstition passed into the more inno
cent one of men having a power to charm wolves.

And of the goblin that came in the night to water the
    horses,
And of the white Létiche, the ghost of a child who
    unchristened
Died, and was doomed to haunt unseen the chambers
    of children ;
And how on Christmas eve the oxen talked in the
    stable,
And how the fever was cured by a spider shut up in
    a nutshell,   285
And of the marvellous powers of four-leaved clover
    and horseshoes,
With whatsoever else was writ in the lore of the village.
Then up rose from his seat by the fireside Basil the
    blacksmith,
Knocked from his pipe the ashes, and slowly extend-
    ing his right hand,
" Father Leblanc," he exclaimed; " thou hast heard
    the talk in the village,   290
And, perchance, canst tell us some news of these ships
    and their errand."
Then with modest demeanor made answer the notary
    public, —
" Gossip enough have I heard, in sooth, yet am never
    the wiser ;

282. Pluquet relates this superstition, and conjectures that the
white, fleet ermine gave rise to it.

284. A belief still lingers among the peasantry of England, as
well as on the Continent, that at midnight, on Christmas eve, the
cattle in the stalls fall down on their knees in adoration of the
infant Saviour, as the old legend says was done in the stable at
Bethlehem.

285. In like manner a popular superstition prevailed in England that ague could be cured by sealing a spider in a goose-
quill and hanging it about the neck.

And what their errand may be I know no better than
    others.
Yet am I not of those who imagine some evil inten-
    tion   295
Brings them here, for we are at peace; and why then
    molest us?"
"God's name!" shouted the hasty and somewhat iras-
    cible blacksmith;
"Must we in all things look for the how, and the why,
    and the wherefore?
Daily injustice is done, and might is the right of the
    strongest!"
But, without heeding his warmth, continued the notary
    public, —   300
"Man is unjust, but God is just; and finally justice
Triumphs; and well I remember a story, that often
    consoled me,
When as a captive I lay in the old French fort at
    Port Royal."
This was the old man's favorite tale, and he loved to
    repeat it
When his neighbors complained that any injustice was
    done them.   305
"Once in an ancient city, whose name I no longer re-
    member,
Raised aloft on a column, a brazen statue of Justice
Stood in the public square, upholding the scales in its
    left hand,
And in its right a sword, as an emblem that justice
    presided
Over the laws of the land, and the hearts and homes
    of the people.   310

302. This is an old Florentine story; in an altered form it is
the theme of Rossini's opera of *La Gazza Ladra.*

Even the birds had built their nests in the scales of
    the balance,
Having no fear of the sword that flashed in the sun-
    shine above them.
But in the course of time the laws of the land were
    corrupted ;
Might took the place of right, and the weak were
    oppressed, and the mighty
Ruled with an iron rod.   Then it chanced in a noble-
    man's palace   315
That a necklace of pearls was lost, and ere long a sus-
    picion
Fell on an orphan girl who lived as a maid in the house-
    hold.
She, after form of trial condemned to die on the scaf-
    fold,
Patiently met her doom at the foot of the statue of
    Justice.
As to her Father in heaven her innocent spirit as-
    cended,   320
Lo! o'er the city a tempest rose ; and the bolts of the
    thunder
Smote the statue of bronze, and hurled in wrath from
    its left hand
Down on the pavement below the clattering scales of
    the balance,
And in the hollow thereof was found the nest of a
    magpie,
Into whose clay-built walls the necklace of pearls was
    inwoven."   325
Silenced, but not convinced, when the story was ended,
    the blacksmith
Stood like a man who fain would speak. but findeth
    no language ;

All his thoughts were congealed into lines on his face, as the vapors
Freeze in fantastic shapes on the window-panes in the winter.

Then Evangeline lighted the brazen lamp on the table, 330
Filled, till it overflowed, the pewter tankard with home-brewed
Nut-brown ale, that was famed for its strength in the village of Grand-Pré;
While from his pocket the notary drew his papers and inkhorn,
Wrote with a steady hand the date and the age of the parties,
Naming the dower of the bride in flocks of sheep and in cattle. 335
Orderly all things proceeded, and duly and well were completed,
And the great seal of the law was set like a sun on the margin.
Then from his leathern pouch the farmer threw on the table
Three times the old man's fee in solid pieces of silver;
And the notary rising, and blessing the bride and bridegroom, 340
Lifted aloft the tankard of ale and drank to their welfare.
Wiping the foam from his lip, he solemnly bowed and departed,
While in silence the others sat and mused by the fireside,

Till Evangeline brought the draught-board out of its
  corner.
Soon was the game begun.   In friendly contention
  the old men   345
Laughed at each lucky hit, or unsuccessful manœuvre,
Laughed when a man was crowned, or a breach was
  made in the king-row.
Meanwhile apart, in the twilight gloom of a window's
  embrasure,
Sat the lovers and whispered together, beholding the
  moon rise
Over the pallid sea and the silvery mists of the mead-
  ows.   350
Silently one by one, in the infinite meadows of heaven,
Blossomed the lovely stars, the forget-me-nots of the
  angels.

Thus was the evening passed.   Anon the bell from
  the belfry
Rang out the hour of nine, the village curfew, and
  straightway
Rose the guests and departed ; and silence reigned in
  the household.   355

344. The word *draughts* is derived from the circumstance of
drawing the men from one square to another.
354. *Curfew* is a corruption of *couvre-feu*, or cover fire   In
the Middle Ages, when police patrol at night was almost unknown, it was attempted to lessen the chances of crime by making it an offence against the laws to be found in the streets in
the night, and the curfew bell was tolled, at various hours, according to the custom of the place, from seven to nine o'clock in
the evening.   It warned honest people to lock their doors, cover
their fires, and go to bed.   The custom still lingers in many
places, even in America, of ringing a bell at nine o'clock in the
evening.

Many a farewell word and sweet good-night on the
door-step
Lingered long in Evangeline's heart, and filled it with
gladness.
Carefully then were covered the embers that glowed
on the hearth-stone,
And on the oaken stairs resounded the tread of the
farmer.
Soon with a soundless step the foot of Evangeline followed.   360
Up the staircase moved a luminous space in the darkness,
Lighted less by the lamp than the shining face of the
maiden.
Silent she passed the hall, and entered the door of her
chamber.
Simple that chamber was, with its curtains of white,
and its clothes-press
Ample and high, on whose spacious shelves were care-
fully folded   365
Linen and woollen stuffs, by the hand of Evangeline
woven.
This was the precious dower she would bring to her
husband in marriage,
Better than flocks and herds, being proofs of her skill
as a housewife.
Soon she extinguished her lamp, for the mellow and
radiant moonlight
Streamed through the windows, and lighted the rocm,
till the heart of the maiden   370
Swelled and obeyed its power, like the tremulous tides
of the ocean.
Ah! she was fair, exceeding fair to behold, as she
stood with

Naked snow-white feet on the gleaming floor of her
    chamber!
Little she dreamed that below, among the trees of the
    orchard,
Waited her lover and watched for the gleam of her
    lamp and her shadow.   375
Yet were her thoughts of him, and at times a feeling
    of sadness
Passed o'er her soul, as the sailing shade of clouds in
    the moonlight
Flitted across the floor and darkened the room for a
    moment.
And, as she gazed from the window, she saw serenely
    the moon pass
Forth from the folds of a cloud, and one star follow
    her footsteps,   380
As out of Abraham's tent young Ishmael wandered
    with Hagar.

IV.

    Pleasantly rose next morn the sun on the village
    of Grand-Pré.
Pleasantly gleamed in the soft, sweet air the Basin of
    Minas,
Where the ships, with their wavering shadows, were
    riding at anchor.
Life had long been astir in the village, and clamorous
    labor   385
Knocked with its hundred hands at the golden gates
    of the morning.
Now from the country around, from the farms and
    neighboring hamlets,
Came in their holiday dresses the blithe Acadian
    peasants.

Many a glad good-morrow and jocund laugh from the
    young folk
Made the bright air brighter, as up from the numer-
    ous meadows,   390
Where no path could be seen but the track of wheels
    in the greensward,
Group after group appeared, and joined, or passed on
    the highway.
Long ere noon, in the village all sounds of labor were
    silenced.
Thronged were the streets with people; and noisy
    groups at the house-doors
Sat in the cheerful sun, and rejoiced and gossiped to-
    gether.   395
Every house was an inn, where all were welcomed and
    feasted;
For with this simple people, who lived like brothers
    together,
All things were held in common, and what one had
    was another's.
Yet under Benedict's roof hospitality seemed more
    abundant:

396. " Real misery was wholly unknown, and benevolence
anticipated the demands of poverty. Every misfortune was relieved as it were before it could be felt, without ostentation on
the one hand, and without meanness on the other. It was, in
short, a society of brethren, every individual of which was
equally ready to give and to receive what he thought the common right of mankind." — From the Abbé Raynal's account of
the Acadians. The Abbé Guillaume Thomas Francis Raynal
was a French writer (1711–1796), who published *A Philosophi-
cal History of the Settlements and Trade of the Europeans in the
East and West Indies*, in which he included also some account of
Canada and Nova Scotia. His picture of life among the Acadians, somewhat highly colored, is the source from which after
writers have drawn their knowledge of Acadian manners.

For Evangeline stood among the guests of her
    father;   400
Bright was her face with smiles, and words of wel-
    come and gladness
Fell from her beautiful lips, and blessed the cup as
    she gave it.

  Under the open sky, in the odorous air of the
    orchard,
Stript of its golden fruit, was spread the feast of be-
    trothal.
There in the shade of the porch were the priest and
    the notary seated;   405
There good Benedict sat, and sturdy Basil the black-
    smith.
Not far withdrawn from these, by the cider-press and
    the beehives,
Michael the fiddler was placed, with the gayest of
    hea.ts and of waistcoats.
Shadow and light from the leaves alternately played
    on his snow-white
Hair, as it waved in the wind; and the jolly face of
    the fiddler   410
Glowed like a living coal when the ashes are blown
    from the embers.
Gayly the old man sang to the vibrant sound of his
    fiddle,
Tous les Bourgeois de Chartres, and *Le Carillon de
    Dunkerque*,

---

413. *Tous les Bourgeois de Chartres* was a song written by
Ducauroi, *maître de chapelle* of Henri IV., the words of which
are : —

Vous connaissez Cybèle,	You remember Cybele,
Qui sut fixer le Temps ;	Wise the seasons to unfold ;
On la disait fort belle,	Very fair, said men, was she,
Même dans ses vieux ans.	Even when her years grew old.

And anon with his wooden shoes beat time to the
    music.

Merrily, merrily whirled the wheels of the dizzying
    dances   415

Under the orchard-trees and down the path to the
    meadows;

Old folk and young together, and children mingled
    among them.

Fairest of all the maids was Evangeline, Benedict's
    daughter!

Noblest of all the youths was Gabriel, son of the
    blacksmith!

So passed the morning away. And lo! with a sum-
    mons sonorous   420

Sounded the bell from its tower, and over the mead-
    ows a drum beat.

Thronged ere long was the church with men. With-
    out, in the churchyard,

CHORUS.	CHORUS.
Cette divinité, quoique déjà grand'mère	A grandame, yet by goddess birth
Avait les yeux doux, le teint frais,	She kept sweet eyes, a color warm,
Avait même certains attraits	And held through everything a charm
Fermes comme la Terre.	Fast like the earth.

Le Carillon de Dunkerque was a popular song to a tune played
on the Dunkirk chimes. The words are : —

Le Carillon de Dunkerque.	*The Carillon of Dunkirk.*
Imprudent, téméraire	Reckless and rash,
A l'instant, je l'espère	Take heed for the flash
Dans mon juste courroux,	Of mine anger, 't is just
Tu vas tomber sous mes coups!	To lay thee with its blows in the dust.
— Je brave ta menace.	— Your threat I defy.
— Etre moi! quelle audace!	— What! You would be I!
Avance donc, poltron!	Come, coward! I 'll show —
Tu trembles? non, non, non.	You tremble? No, no!
— J'étouffe de colère!	— I 'm choking with rage!
— Je ris de ta colère.	— A fig for your rage!

The music to which the old man sang these songs will be found
in *La Clé du Caveau*, by Pierre Capelle, Nos. 564 and 739.
Paris : A. Cotelle.

Waited the women. They stood by the graves, and
    hung on the headstones
Garlands of autumn-leaves and evergreens fresh from
    the forest.
Then came the guard from the ships, and marching
    proudly among them   425
Entered the sacred portal. With loud and dissonant
    clangor
Echoed the sound of their brazen drums from ceiling
    and casement, —
Echoed a moment only, and slowly the ponderous por-
    tal
Closed, and in silence the crowd awaited the will of
    the soldiers.
Then uprose their commander, and spake from the
    steps of the altar,   430
Holding aloft in his hands, with its seals, the royal
    commission.
" You are convened this day," he said, " by his Maj-
    esty's orders.
Clement and kind has he been; but how you have
    answered his kindness
Let your own hearts reply! To my natural make and
    my temper
Painful the task is I do, which to you I know must
    be grievous.   435
Yet must I bow and obey, and deliver the will of our
    monarch :
Namely, that all your lands, and dwellings, and cattle
    of all kinds
Forfeited be to the crown ; and that you yourselves
    from this province

    432. Colonel Winslow has preserved in his Diary the speech
which he delivered to the assembled Acadians, and it is copied
by Haliburton in his *History of Nova Scotia*, i. 166, 167.

Be transported to other lands. God grant you may
    dwell there
Ever as faithful subjects, a happy and peaceable peo-
    ple!   440
Prisoners now I declare you, for such is his Majesty's
    pleasure!"
As, when the air is serene in the sultry solstice of
    summer,
Suddenly gathers a storm, and the deadly sling of the
    hailstones
Beats down the farmer's corn in the field, and shatters
    his windows,
Hiding the sun, and strewing the ground with thatch
    from the house-roofs,   445
Bellowing fly the herds, and seek to break their en-
    closures;
So on the hearts of the people descended the words of
    the speaker.
Silent a moment they stood in speechless wonder, and
    then rose
Louder and ever louder a wail of sorrow and anger,
And, by one impulse moved, they madly rushed to the
    door-way.   450
Vain was the hope of escape; and cries and fierce
    imprecations
Rang through the house of prayer; and high o'er the
    heads of the others
Rose, with his arms uplifted, the figure of Basil the
    blacksmith,
As, on a stormy sea, a spar is tossed by the billows.
Flushed was his face and distorted with passion; and
    wildly he shouted, —   455
"Down with the tyrants of England! we never have
    sworn them allegiance!

Death to these foreign soldiers, who seize on our
    homes and our harvests ! ''
More he fain would have said, but the merciless hand
    of a soldier
Smote him upon the mouth, and dragged him down to
    the pavement.

In the midst of the strife and tumult of angry con-
    tention,   460
Lo ! the door of the chancel opened, and Father Feli-
    cian
Entered, with serious mien, and ascended the steps of
    the altar.
Raising his reverend hand, with a gesture he awed
    into silence
All that clamorous throng ; and thus he spake to his
    people ;
Deep were his tones and solemn ; in accents measured
    and mournful   465
Spake he, as, after the tocsin's alarum, distinctly the
    clock strikes.
" What is this that ye do, my children ? what madness
    has seized you ?
Forty years of my life have I labored among you, and
    taught you,
Not in word alone, but in deed, to love one another !
Is this the fruit of my toils, of my vigils and prayers
    and privations ?   470
Have you so soon forgotten all lessons of love and
    forgiveness ?
This is the house of the Prince of Peace, and would
    you profane it
Thus with violent deeds and hearts overflowing with
    hatred ?

Lo! where the crucified Christ from His cross is gaz-
 ing upon you!
See! in those sorrowful eyes what meekness and holy
 compassion! 475
Hark! how those lips still repeat the prayer, 'O
 Father, forgive them!'
Let us repeat that prayer in the hour when the wicked
 assail us,
Let us repeat it now, and say, 'O Father, forgive
 them!'"
Few were his words of rebuke, but deep in the hearts
 of his people
Sank they, and sobs of contrition succeeded the pas-
 sionate outbreak, 480
While they repeated his prayer, and said, "O Father,
 forgive them!"

Then came the evening service. The tapers gleamed
 from the altar;
Fervent and deep was the voice of the priest, and the
 people responded,
Not with their lips alone, but their hearts; and the
 Ave Maria
Sang they, and fell on their knees, and their souls,
 with devotion translated, 485
Rose on the ardor of prayer, like Elijah ascending to
 heaven.

Meanwhile had spread in the village the tidings of
 ill, and on all sides
Wandered, wailing, from house to house the women
 and children.
Long at her father's door Evangeline stood, with her
 right hand

Shielding her eyes from the level rays of the sun,
that, descending,   490
Lighted the village street with mysterious splendor,
and roofed each
Peasant's cottage with golden thatch, and emblazoned
its windows.
Long within had been spread the snow-white cloth on
the table ;
There stood the wheaten loaf, and the honey fragrant
with wild flowers ;
There stood the tankard of ale, and the cheese fresh
brought from the dairy ;   .   495
And at the head of the board the great arm-chair of
the farmer.
Thus did Evangeline wait at her father's door, as the
sunset
Threw the long shadows of trees o'er the broad am-
brosial meadows.
Ah ! on her spirit within a deeper shadow had fallen,
And from the fields of her soul a fragrance celestial
ascended, —   500
Charity, meekness, love, and hope, and forgiveness,
and patience !
Then, all forgetful of self, she wandered into the vil-
lage,
Cheering with looks and words the mournful hearts of
the women,
As o'er the darkening fields with lingering steps they
departed,
Urged by their household cares, and the weary feet of
their children.   505

492. To emblazon is literally to adorn anything with ensigns
armorial.   It was often the custom to work these ensigns into
the design of painted windows.

Down sank the great red sun, and in golden, glimmer-
    ing vapors
Veiled the light of his face, like the Prophet descend-
    ing from Sinai.
Sweetly over the village the bell of the Angelus
    sounded.

    Meanwhile, amid the gloom, by the church Evange-
    line lingered.
All was silent within; and in vain at the door and the
    windows   510
Stood she, and listened and looked, until, overcome by
    emotion,
"Gabriel!" cried she aloud with tremulous voice;
    but no answer
Came from the graves of the dead, nor the gloomier
    grave of the living.
Slowly at length she returned to the tenantless house
    of her father.
Smouldered the fire on the hearth, on the board was
    the supper untasted.   515
Empty and drear was each room, and haunted with
    phantoms of terror.
Sadly echoed her step on the stair and the floor of her
    chamber.
In the dead of the night she heard the disconsolate
    rain fall
Loud on the withered leaves of the sycamore-tree by
    the window.
Keenly the lightning flashed; and the voice of the
    echoing thunder   520
Told her that God was in heaven, and governed the
    world He created!

Then she remembered the tale she had heard of the
    justice of Heaven ;
Soothed was her troubled soul, and she peacefully
    slumbered till morning.

v.

Four times the sun had risen and set ; and now on
    the fifth day
Cheerily called the cock to the sleeping maids of the
    farm-house.   525
Soon o'er the yellow fields, in silent and mournful pro-
    cession,
Came from the neighboring hamlets and farms the
    Acadian women,
Driving in ponderous wains their household goods to
    the sea-shore,
Pausing and looking back to gaze once more on their
    dwellings,
Ere they were shut from sight by the winding road and
    the woodland.   530
Close at their sides their children ran, and urged on
    the oxen,
While in their little hands they clasped some frag-
    ments of playthings.

Thus to the Gaspereau's mouth they hurried ; and
    there on the sea-beach
Piled in confusion lay the household goods of the
    peasants.
All day long between the shore and the ships did the
    boats ply ;   535
All day long the wains came laboring down from the
    village.
Late in the afternoon, when the sun was near to his
    setting,

Echoed far o'er the fields came the roll of drums from
    the churchyard.
Thither the women and children thronged. On a sud-
    den the church-doors
Opened, and forth came the guard, and marching in
    gloomy procession   540
Followed the long-imprisoned, but patient, Acadian
    farmers.
Even as pilgrims, who journey afar from their homes
    and their country,
Sing as they go, and in singing forget they are weary
    and wayworn,
So with songs on their lips the Acadian peasants de-
    scended
Down from the church to the shore, amid their wives
    and their daughters.   545
Foremost the young men came ; and, raising together
    their voices,
Sang with tremulous lips a chant of the Catholic
    Missions : —
" Sacred heart of the Saviour ! O inexhaustible foun
    tain !
Fill our hearts this day with strength and submission
    and patience ! "
Then the old men, as they marched, and the women
    that stood by the wayside   550
Joined in the sacred psalm, and the birds in the sun-
    shine above them
Mingled their notes therewith, like voices of spirits
    departed.

    Half-way down to the shore Evangeline waited in
    silence,
Not overcome with grief, but strong in the hour of
    affliction. —

Calmly and sadly she waited, until the procession ap-
    proached her,   555
And she beheld the face of Gabriel pale with emotion.
Tears then filled her eyes, and, eagerly running to
    meet him,
Clasped she his hands, and laid her head on his
    shoulder, and whispered, —
"Gabriel! be of good cheer! for if we love one
    another
Nothing, in truth, can harm us, whatever mischances
    may happen!"   560
Smiling she spake these words; then suddenly paused,
    for her father
Saw she, slowly advancing.   Alas! how changed was
    his aspect!
Gone was the glow from his cheek, and the fire from
    his eye, and his footstep
Heavier seemed with the weight of the heavy heart
    in his bosom.
But with a smile and a sigh, she clasped his neck and
    embraced him,   565
Speaking words of endearment where words of com-
    fort availed not.
Thus to the Gaspereau's mouth moved on that mourn-
    ful procession.

    There disorder prevailed, and the tumult and stir of
    embarking.
Busily plied the freighted boats; and in the confusion
Wives were torn from their husbands, and mothers,
    too late, saw their children   570
Left on the land, extending their arms, with wildest
    entreaties.
So unto separate ships were Basil and Gabriel carried,

While in despair on the shore Evangeline stood with
    her father.

Half the task was not done when the sun went down,
    and the twilight

Deepened and darkened around; and in haste the
    refluent ocean   575

Fled away from the shore, and left the line of the
    sand-beach

Covered with waifs of the tide, with kelp and the slip-
    pery sea-weed.

Farther back in the midst of the household goods and
    the wagons,

Like to a gypsy camp, or a leaguer after a battle,

All escape cut off by the sea, and the sentinels near
    them,   580

Lay encamped for the night the houseless Acadian
    farmers.

Back to its nethermost caves retreated the bellowing
    ocean,

Dragging adown the beach the rattling pebbles, and
    leaving

Inland and far up the shore the stranded boats of the
    sailors.

Then, as the night descended, the herds returned from
    their pastures;   585

Sweet was the moist still air with the odor of milk
    from their udders;

Lowing they waited, and long, at the well-known bars
    of the farm-yard, —

Waited and looked in vain for the voice and the hand
    of the milkmaid.

Silence reigned in the streets; from the church no
    Angelus sounded,

Rose no smoke from the roofs, and gleamed no lights
    from the windows.   590

But on the shores meanwhile the evening fires had
    been kindled,
Built of the drift-wood thrown on the sands from
    wrecks in the tempest.
Round them shapes of gloom and sorrowful faces were
    gathered,
Voices of women were heard, and of men, and the
    crying of children.
Onward from fire to fire, as from hearth to hearth in
    his parish,   595
Wandered the faithful priest, consoling and blessing
    and cheering,
Like unto shipwrecked Paul on Melita's desolate sea-
    shore.
Thus he approached the place where Evangeline sat
    with her father,
And in the flickering light beheld the face of the old
    man,
Haggard and hollow and wan, and without either
    thought or emotion,   600
E'en as the face of a clock from which the hands have
    been taken.
Vainly Evangeline strove with words and caresses to
    cheer him,
Vainly offered him food : yet he moved not, he looked
    not, he spake not,
But, with a vacant stare, ever gazed at the flickering
    fire-light.
" *Benedicite !* " murmured the priest, in tones of com-
    passion.   605
More he fain would have said, but his heart was full,
    and his accents
Faltered and paused on his lips, as the feet of a child
    on a threshold,

Hushed by the scene he beholds, and the awful presence of sorrow.
Silently, therefore, he laid his hand on the head of the
maiden,
Raising his tearful eyes to the silent stars that above
them   610
Moved on their way, unperturbed by the wrongs and
sorrows of mortals.
Then sat he down at her side, and they wept together
in silence.

Suddenly rose from the south a light, as in autumn
the blood-red
Moon climbs the crystal walls of heaven, and o'er the
horizon
Titan-like stretches its hundred hands upon mountain
and meadow,   615
Seizing the rocks and the rivers, and piling huge
shadows together.
Broader and ever broader it gleamed on the roofs of
the village,
Gleamed on the sky and sea, and the ships that lay in
the roadstead.
Columns of shining smoke uprose, and flashes of
flame were
Thrust through their folds and withdrawn, like the
quivering hands of a martyr.   620

615. The Titans were giant deities in Greek mythology who
attempted to deprive Saturn of the sovereignty of heaven, and
were driven down into Tartarus by Jupiter, the son of Saturn,
who hurled thunderbolts at them Briareus, the hundred-handed
giant, was in mythology of the same parentage as the Titans,
but was not classed with them

Then as the wind seized the gleeds and the burning
    thatch, and, uplifting,
Whirled them aloft through the air, at once from a
    hundred house-tops
Started the sheeted smoke with flashes of flame inter-
    mingled.

These things beheld in dismay the crowd on the
    shore and on shipboard.
Speechless at first they stood, then cried aloud in their
    anguish,   625
" We shall behold no more our homes in the village of
    Grand-Pré ! "
Loud on a sudden the cocks began to crow in the farm-
    yards,
Thinking the day had dawned ; and anon the lowing
    of cattle
Came on the evening breeze, by the barking of dogs
    interrupted.
Then rose a sound of dread, such as startles the sleep-
    ing encampments   630
Far in the western prairies of forests that skirt the
    Nebraska,
When the wild horses affrighted sweep by with the
    speed of the whirlwind,

621. *Gleeds.* Hot, burning coals ; a Chaucerian word : —
    " And wafres piping hoot out of the gleede."
                    Canterbury Tales, l. 3379.

The burning of the houses was in accordance with the instruc-
tions of the Governor to Colonel Winslow, in case he should fail
in collecting all the inhabitants : " You must proceed by the most
vigorous measures possible, not only in compelling them to em-
bark, but in depriving those who shall escape of all means of
shelter or support, by burning their houses and by destroying
everything that may afford them the means of subsistence in the
country."

Or the loud bellowing herds of buffaloes rush to the
    river.
Such was the sound that arose on the night, as the
    herds and the horses
Broke through their folds and fences, and madly
    rushed o'er the meadows.   635

  Overwhelmed with the sight, yet speechless, the
    priest and the maiden
Gazed on the scene of terror that reddened and
    widened before them ;
And as they turned at length to speak to their silent
    companion,
Lo! from his seat he had fallen, and stretched abroad
    on the seashore
Motionless lay his form, from which the soul had de-
    parted.   640
Slowly the priest uplifted the lifeless head, and the
    maiden
Knelt at her father's side, and wailed aloud in her
    terror.
Then in a swoon she sank, and lay with her head on
    his bosom.
Through the long night she lay in deep, oblivious
    slumber ;
And when she woke from the trance, she beheld a
    multitude near her.   645
Faces of friends she beheld, that were mournfully gaz-
    ing upon her,
Pallid, with tearful eyes, and looks of saddest com-
    passion.
Still the blaze of the burning village illumined the
    landscape,

Reddened the sky overhead, and gleamed on the faces
  around her,

And like the day of doom it seemed to her wavering
  senses.   650

Then a familiar voice she heard, as it said to the people, —

" Let us bury him here by the sea.   When a happier
  season

Brings us again to our homes from the unknown land
  of our exile,

Then shall his sacred dust be piously laid in the
  churchyard."

Such were the words of the priest.   And there in
  haste by the sea-side,   655

Having the glare of the burning village for funeral
  torches,

But without bell or book, they buried the farmer of
  Grand-Pré.

And as the voice of the priest repeated the service of
  sorrow,

Lo! with a mournful sound like the voice of a vast
  congregation,

Solemnly answered the sea, and mingled its roar with
  the dirges.   660

'T was the returning tide, that afar from the waste of
  the ocean,

With the first dawn of the day, came heaving and hur-
  rying landward.

Then recommenced once more the stir and noise of
  embarking ;

657. The bell was tolled to mark the passage of the soul into
the other world ; the book was the service book.   The phrase
"bell, book, or candle " was used in referring to excommunica-
tion.

And with the ebb of the tide the ships sailed out of
    the harbor,
Leaving behind them the dead on the shore, and the
    village in ruins.   66ª

PART THE SECOND.

I.

MANY a weary year had passed since the burning of
    Grand-Pré,
When on the falling tide the freighted vessels de-
    parted,
Bearing a nation, with all its household gods, into
    exile,
Exile without an end, and without an example in
    story.
Far asunder, on separate coasts, the Acadians
    landed;   670
Scattered were they, like flakes of snow, when the
    wind from the northeast
Strikes aslant through the fogs that darken the Banks
    of Newfoundland.
Friendless, homeless, hopeless, they wandered from
    city to city,
From the cold lakes of the North to sultry Southern
    savannas, —
From the bleak shores of the sea to the lands where
    the Father of Waters   67č
Seizes the hills in his hands, and drags them down to
    the ocean,
Deep in their sands to bury the scattered bones of the
    mammoth.

    677. Bones of the mastodon, or mammoth, have been found

Friends they sought and homes; and many, despairing,
    heart-broken,
Asked of the earth but a grave, and no longer a friend
    nor a fireside.
Written their history stands on tablets of stone in the
    churchyards.   630
Long among them was seen a maiden who waited and
    wandered,
Lowly and meek in spirit, and patiently suffering all
    things.
Fair was she and young; but, alas! before her ex-
    tended,
Dreary and vast and silent, the desert of life, with its
    pathway
Marked by the graves of those who had sorrowed and
    suffered before her,   635
Passions long extinguished, and hopes long dead and
    abandoned,
As the emigrant's way o'er the Western desert is
    marked by
Camp-fires long consumed, and bones that bleach in
    the sunshine.
Something there was in her life incomplete, imperfect,
    unfinished;
As if a morning of June, with all its music and sun-
    shine,   690
Suddenly paused in the sky, and, fading, slowly de-
    scended
Into the east again, from whence it late had arisen.
Sometimes she lingered in towns, till, urged by the
    fever within her,

scattered all over the territory of the United States and Canada,
but the greatest number have been collected in the Salt Licks of
Kentucky, and in the States of Ohio, Mississippi, Missouri, and
Alabama.

Urged by a restless longing, the hunger and thirst of
    the spirit,

She would commence again her endless search and en-
    deavor ;   695

Sometimes in churchyards strayed, and gazed on the
    crosses and tombstones,

Sat by some nameless grave, and thought that perhaps
    in its bosom

He was already at rest, and she longed to slumber be-
    side him.

Sometimes a rumor, a hearsay, an inarticulate whis-
    per,

Came with its airy hand to point and beckon her for-
    ward.   700

Sometimes she spake with those who had seen her be-
    loved and known him,

But it was long ago, in some far-off place or forgot-
    ten.

" Gabriel Lajeunesse ! " they said ; " Oh, yes ! we have
    seen him.

He was with Basil the blacksmith, and both have gone
    to the prairies ;

Coureurs-des-bois are they, and famous hunters and
    trappers."   705

699. Observe the diminution in this line, by which one is led
to the *airy hand* in the next.

705. The *coureurs-des-bois* formed a class of men, very early in
Canadian history, produced by the exigencies of the fur-trade.
They were French by birth, but by long affiliation with the Indians and adoption of their customs had become half-civilized
vagrants, whose chief vocation was conducting the canoes of the
traders along the lakes and rivers of the interior. *Bushrangers*
is the English equivalent. They played an important part in the
Indian wars, but were nearly as lawless as the Indians themselves. The reader will find them frequently referred to in

"Gabriel Lajeunesse!" said others; "Oh, yes! we
    have seen him.
He is a voyageur in the lowlands of Louisiana."
Then would they say, "Dear child! why dream and
    wait for him longer?
Are there not other youths as fair as Gabriel? others
Who have hearts as tender and true, and spirits as
    loyal?   710
Here is Baptiste Leblanc, the notary's son, who has
    loved thee
Many a tedious year; come, give him thy hand and be
    happy!
Thou art too fair to be left to braid St. Catherine's
    tresses."
Then would Evangeline answer, serenely but sadly,
    "I cannot!
Whither my heart has gone, there follows my hand,
    and not elsewhere.   715
For when the heart goes before, like a lamp, and
    illumines the pathway,
Many things are made clear, that else lie hidden in
    darkness."
Thereupon the priest, her friend and father confessor,
Said, with a smile, "O daughter! thy God thus
    speaketh within thee!
Talk not of wasted affection, affection never was
    wasted;   720

Parkman's histories, especially in *The Conspiracy of Pontiac,*
The Discovery of the Great West, and *Frontenac and New France*
under Louis XIV.

707. A *voyageur* is a river boatman, and is a term applied
usually to Canadians.

713. St. Catherine of Alexandria and St. Catherine of Siena
were both celebrated for their vows of virginity. Hence the saying *to braid St. Catherine's tresses,* of one devoted to a single life.

If it enrich not the heart of another, its waters, returning
Back to their springs, like the rain, shall fill them full
of refreshment ;
That which the fountain sends forth returns again to
the fountain.
Patience ; accomplish thy labor ; accomplish thy work
of affection !
Sorrow and silence are strong, and patient endurance
is godlike. ⁷²⁵
Therefore accomplish thy labor of love, till the heart
is made godlike,
Purified, strengthened, perfected, and rendered more
worthy of heaven ! "
Cheered by the good man's words, Evangeline labored
and waited.
Still in her heart she heard the funeral dirge of the
ocean,
But with its sound there was mingled a voice that
whispered, " Despair not ! " ⁷³⁰
Thus did that poor soul wander in want and cheer-
less discomfort,
Bleeding, barefooted, over the shards and thorns of
existence.
Let me essay, O Muse ! to follow the wanderer's footsteps ; —
Not through each devious path, each changeful year
of existence ;
But as a traveller follows a streamlet's course through
the valley : ⁷³⁵
Far from its margin at times, and seeing the gleam of
its water
Here and there, in some open space, and at intervals
only ;

Then drawing nearer its banks, through sylvan glooms
 that conceal it,
Though he behold it not, he can hear its continuous
 murmur;
Happy, at length, if he find a spot where it reaches
 an outlet.   74ʹ

II.

It was the month of May. Far down the Beautiful
 River,
Past the Ohio shore and past the mouth of the Wa-
 bash,
Into the golden stream of the broad and swift Mis-
 sissippi,
Floated a cumbrous boat, that was rowed by Acadian
 boatmen.
It was a band of exiles: a raft, as it were, from the
 shipwrecked   745
Nation, scattered along the coast, now floating to-
 gether,
Bound by the bonds of a common belief and a com-
 mon misfortune;
Men and women and children, who, guided by hope
 or by hearsay,
Sought for their kith and their kin among the few-
 acred farmers
On the Acadian coast, and the prairies of fair Opelousas.   75(

---

741. The Iroquois gave to this river the name of Ohio, or the
Beautiful River, and La Salle, who was the first European to
discover it, preserved the name, so that it was transferred to
maps very early.

750. Between the 1st of January and the 13th of May, 1765,
about six hundred and fifty Acadians had arrived at New Or-

With them Evangeline went, and her guide, the
    Father Felician.

Onward o'er sunken sands, through a wilderness
    sombre with forests,

Day after day they glided adown the turbulent river ;

Night after night, by their blazing fires, encamped on
    its borders.

Now through rushing chutes, among green islands,
    where plumelike   755

Cotton-trees nodded their shadowy crests, they swept
    with the current,

Then emerged into broad lagoons, where silvery sand-
    bars

Lay in the stream, and along the wimpling waves of
    their margin,

Shining with snow-white plumes, large flocks of pel-
    icans waded.

Level the landscape grew, and along the shores of the
    river,   760

Shaded by china-trees, in the midst of luxuriant gar-
    dens,

Stood the houses of planters, with negro cabins and
    dove-cots.

They were approaching the region where reigns per-
    petual summer,

leans. Louisiana had been ceded by France to Spain in 1762
but did not really pass under the control of the Spanish until
1769. The existence of a French population attracted the wandering Acadians, and they were sent by the authorities to form
settlements in Attakapas and Opelousas. They afterward formed
settlements on both sides of the Mississippi from the German
Coast up to Baton Rouge, and even as high as Pointe Coupée.
Hence the name of Acadian Coast, which a portion of the banks
of the river still bears. See Gayarré's *History of Louisiana :
The French Dominion,* vol. ii.

Where through the Golden Coast, and groves of
    orange and citron,
Sweeps with majestic curve the river away to the east-
    ward.   765
They, too, swerved from their course; and, entering
    the Bayou of Plaquemine,
Soon were lost in a maze of sluggish and devious
    waters,
Which, like a network of steel, extended in every
    direction.
Over their heads the towering and tenebrous boughs
    of the cypress
Met in a dusky arch, and trailing mosses in mid-
    air   770
Waved like banners that hang on the walls of ancient
    cathedrals.
Deathlike the silence seemed, and unbroken, save by
    the herons
Home to their roosts in the cedar-trees returning at
    sunset,
Or by the owl, as he greeted the moon with demoniac
    laughter.
Lovely the moonlight was as it glanced and gleamed
    on the water,   775
Gleamed on the columns of cypress and cedar sustain-
    ing the arches,
Down through whose broken vaults it fell as through
    chinks in a ruin.
Dreamlike, and indistinct, and strange were all things
    around them;
And o'er their spirits there came a feeling of wonder
    and sadness, —
Strange forebodings of ill, unseen and that cannot be
    compassed.

As, at the tramp of a horse's hoof on the turf of the
    prairies,
Far in advance are closed the leaves of the shrinking
    mimosa,
So, at the hoof-beats of fate, with sad forebodings of
    evil,
Shrinks and closes the heart, ere the stroke of doom
    has attained it.
But Evangeline's heart was sustained by a vision, that
    faintly   785
Floated before her eyes, and beckoned her on through
    the moonlight.
It was the thought of her brain that assumed the
    shape of a phantom.
Through those shadowy aisles had Gabriel wandered
    before her,
And every stroke of the oar now brought him nearer
    and nearer.

  Then in his place, at the prow of the boat, rose one
    of the oarsmen,   790
And, as a signal sound, if others like them peradven-
    ture
Sailed on those gloomy and midnight streams, blew a
    blast on his bugle.
Wild through the dark colonnades and corridors leafy
    the blast rang,
Breaking the seal of silence and giving tongues to the
    forest.
Soundless above them the banners of moss just stirred
    to the music.   795
Multitudinous echoes awoke and died in the distance,
Over the watery floor, and beneath the reverberant
    branches ;

But not a voice replied; no answer came from the
    darkness;
And when the echoes had ceased, like a sense of pain
    was the silence.
Then Evangeline slept; but the boatmen rowed
    through the midnight,   800
Silent at times, then singing familiar Canadian boat-
    songs,
Such as they sang of old on their own Acadian rivers,
While through the night were heard the mysterious
    sounds of the desert,
Far off, — indistinct, — as of wave or wind in the
    forest,
Mixed with the whoop of the crane and the roar of
    the grim alligator.   805

    Thus ere another noon they emerged from the
    shades; and before them
Lay, in the golden sun, the lakes of the Atchafalaya.
Water-lilies in myriads rocked on the slight undula-
    tions
Made by the passing oars, and, resplendent in beauty,
    the lotus
Lifted her golden crown above the heads of the boat-
    men.   810
Faint was the air with the odorous breath of magno-
    lia blossoms,
And with the heat of noon; and numberless sylvan
    islands,
Fragrant and thickly embowered with blossoming
    hedges of roses,
Near to whose shores they glided along, invited to
    slumber.
Soon by the fairest of these their weary oars were sus-
    pended.   815

Under the boughs of Wachita willows, that grew by
    the margin,
Safely their boat was moored ; and scattered about on
    the greensward,
Tired with their midnight toil, the weary travellers
    slumbered.
Over them vast and high extended the cope of a
    cedar.
Swinging from its great arms, the trumpet-flower and
    the grapevine   820
Hung their ladder of ropes aloft like the ladder of
    Jacob,
On whose pendulous stairs the angels ascending, de-
    scending,
Were the swift humming-birds, that flitted from blos-
    som to blossom.
Such was the vision Evangeline saw as she slumbered
    beneath it.
Filled was her heart with love, and the dawn of an
    opening heaven   825
Lighted her soul in sleep with the glory of regions
    celestial.

   Nearer, ever nearer, among the numberless islands,
Darted a light, swift boat, that sped away o'er the
    water,
Urged on its course by the sinewy arms of hunters
    and trappers.
Northward its prow was turned, to the land of the
    bison and beaver.   830
At the helm sat a youth, with countenance thoughtful
    and careworn.
Dark and neglected locks overshadowed his brow, and
    a sadness

Somewhat beyond his years on his face was legibly
    written.
Gabriel was it, who, weary with waiting, unhappy and
    restless,
Sought in the Western wilds oblivion of self and of
    sorrow.   835
Swiftly they glided along, close under the lee of the
    island,
But by the opposite bank, and behind a screen of pal-
    mettos ;
So that they saw not the boat, where it lay concealed
    in the willows ;
All undisturbed by the dash of their oars, and unseen,
    were the sleepers ;
Angel of God was there none to awaken the slumber-
    ing maiden.   840
Swiftly they glided away, like the shade of a cloud on
    the prairie.
After the sound of their oars on the tholes had died
    in the distance,
As from a magic trance the sleepers awoke, and the
    maiden
Said with a sigh to the friendly priest, "O Father
    Felician!
Something says in my heart that near me Gabriel
    wanders.   845
Is it a foolish dream, an idle and vague superstition?
Or has an angel passed, and revealed the truth to my
    spirit?"
Then, with a blush, she added, "Alas for my credu-
    lous fancy!
Unto ears like thine such words as these have no
    meaning."
But made answer the reverend man, and he smiled as
    he answered, —   850

" Daughter, thy words are not idle ; nor are they to
    me without meaning,
Feeling is deep and still ; and the word that floats on
    the surface
Is as the tossing buoy, that betrays where the anchor
    is hidden.
Therefore trust to thy heart, and to what the world
    calls illusions.
Gabriel truly is near thee ; for not far away to the
    southward,   855
On the banks of the Têche, are the towns of St. Maur
    and St. Martin.
There the long-wandering bride shall be given again
    to her bridegroom,
There the long-absent pastor regain his flock and his
    sheepfold.
Beautiful is the land, with its prairies and forests of
    fruit-trees ;
Under the feet a garden of flowers, and the bluest of
    heavens   860
Bending above, and resting its dome on the walls of
    the forest.
They who dwell there have named it the Eden of
    Louisiana."

  With these words of cheer they arose and continued
    their journey.
Softly the evening came. The sun from the western
    horizon
Like a magician extended his golden wand o'er the
    landscape ;   865
Twinkling vapors arose ; and sky and water and forest
Seemed all on fire at the touch, and melted and min-
    gled together.

Hanging between two skies, a cloud with edges of
    silver,
Floated the boat, with its dripping oars, on the mo-
    tionless water.
Filled was Evangeline's heart with inexpressible sweet-
    ness.   870
Touched by the magic spell, the sacred fountains of
    feeling
Glowed with the light of love, as the skies and waters
    around her.
Then from a neighboring thicket the mocking-bird,
    wildest of singers,
Swinging aloft on a willow spray that hung o'er the
    water,
Shook from his little throat such floods of delirious
    music,   875
That the whole air and the woods and the waves
    seemed silent to listen.
Plaintive at first were the tones and sad ; then soaring
    to madness
Seemed they to follow or guide the revel of frenzied
    Bacchantes.
Single notes were then heard, in sorrowful, low lam-
    entation ;
Till, having gathered them all, he flung them abroad
    in derision,   880
As when, after a storm, a gust of wind through the
    tree-tops
Shakes down the rattling rain in a crystal shower on
    the branches.

878. The Bacchantes were worshippers of the god Bacchus,
who in Greek mythology presided over the vine and its fruits.
They gave themselves up to all manner of excess, and their
songs and dances were to wild, intoxicating measures.

With such a prelude as this, and hearts that throbbed
    with emotion,
Slowly they entered the Têche, where it flows through
    the green Opelousas,
And, through the amber air, above the crest of the
    woodland, 885
Saw the column of smoke that arose from a neighbor-
    ing dwelling ; —
Sounds of a horn they heard, and the distant lowing
    of cattle.

III.

Near to the bank of the river, o'ershadowed by oaks
    from whose branches
Garlands of Spanish moss and of mystic mistletoe
    flaunted,
Such as the Druids cut down with golden hatchets at
    Yule-tide, 890
Stood, secluded and still, the house of the herdsman.
    A garden
Girded it round about with a belt of luxuriant blos-
    soms,
Filling the air with fragrance. The house itself was
    of timbers
Hewn from the cypress-tree, and carefully fitted to-
    gether.
Large and low was the roof ; and on slender columns
    supported, 895
Rose-wreathed, vine-encircled, a broad and spacious
    veranda,
Haunt of the humming-bird and the bee, extended
    around it.
At each end of the house, amid the flowers of the
    garden,

Stationed the dove-cots were, as love's perpetual sym-
    bol,
Scenes of endless wooing, and endless contentions of
    rivals.   900
Silence reigned o'er the place.   The line of shadow
    and sunshine
Ran near the tops of the trees; but the house itself
    was in shadow,
And from its chimney-top, ascending and slowly ex-
    panding
Into the evening air, a thin blue column of smoke
    rose.
In the rear of the house, from the garden gate, ran a
    pathway   905
Through the great groves of oak to the skirts of the
    limitless prairie,
Into whose sea of flowers the sun was slowly descend-
    ing.
Full in his track of light, like ships with shadowy
    canvas
Hanging loose from their spars in a motionless calm
    in the tropics,
Stood a cluster of trees, with tangled cordage of
    grapevines.   910

    Just where the woodlands met the flowery surf of
        the prairie,
Mounted upon his horse, with Spanish saddle and
    stirrups,
Sat a herdsman, arrayed in gaiters and doublet of
    deerskin.
Broad and brown was the face that from under the
    Spanish sombrero
Gazed on the peaceful scene, with the lordly look of
    its master.   915

Round about him were numberless herds of kine that
    were grazing
Quietly in the meadows, and breathing the vapory
    freshness
That uprose from the river, and spread itself over the
    landscape.
Slowly lifting the horn that hung at his side, and ex-
    panding
Fully his broad, deep chest, he blew a blast, that re-
    sounded   920
Wildly and sweet and far, through the still damp air
    of the evening.
Suddenly out of the grass the long white horns of the
    cattle
Rose like flakes of foam on the adverse currents of
    ocean.
Silent a moment they gazed, then bellowing rushed
    o'er the prairie,
And the whole mass became a cloud, a shade in the
    distance.   925
Then, as the herdsman turned to the house, through
    the gate of the garden
Saw he the forms of the priest and the maiden ad-
    vancing to meet him.
Suddenly down from his horse he sprang in amaze-
    ment, and forward
Pushed with extended arms and exclamations of won-
    der;
When they beheld his face, they recognized Basil the
    blacksmith.   930
Hearty his welcome was, as he led his guests to the
    garden.
There in an arbor of roses with endless question and
    answer

Gave they vent to their hearts, and renewed their
    friendly embraces,
Laughing and weeping by turns, or sitting silent and
    thoughtful.
Thoughtful, for Gabriel came not; and now dark
    doubts and misgivings   935
Stole o'er the maiden's heart; and Basil, somewhat
    embarrassed,
Broke the silence and said, "If you came by the
    Atchafalaya,
How have you nowhere encountered my Gabriel's
    boat on the bayous?"
Over Evangeline's face at the words of Basil a shade
    passed.
Tears came into her eyes, and she said, with a trem-
    ulous accent,   940
"Gone? is Gabriel gone?" and, concealing her face
    on his shoulder,
All her o'erburdened heart gave way, and she wept
    and lamented.
Then the good Basil said, — and his voice grew blithe
    as he said it, —
"Be of good cheer, my child; it is only to-day he
    departed.
Foolish boy! he has left me alone with my herds and
    my horses.   945
Moody and restless grown, and tried and troubled, his
    spirit
Could no longer endure the calm of this quiet exis-
    tence.
Thinking ever of thee, uncertain and sorrowful ever,
Ever silent, or speaking only of thee and his troubles,
He at length had become so tedious to men and to
    maidens,   950

Tedious even to me, that at length I bethought me, and
    sent him
Unto the town of Adayes to trade for mules with the
    Spaniards.
Thence he will follow the Indian trails to the Ozark
    Mountains,
Hunting for furs in the forests, on rivers trapping the
    beaver.
Therefore be of good cheer; we will follow the fugi-
    tive lover;   955
He is not far on his way, and the Fates and the
    streams are against him.
Up and away to-morrow, and through the red dew of
    the morning,
We will follow him fast, and bring him back to his
    prison."

  Then glad voices were heard, and up from the
    banks of the river,
Borne aloft on his comrades' arms, came Michael the
    fiddler.   960
Long under Basil's roof had he lived, like a god on
    Olympus,
Having no other care than dispensing music to mor-
    tals.
Far renowned was he for his silver locks and his
    fiddle.
' Long live Michael," they cried, "our brave Acadian
    minstrel!"
As they bore him aloft in triumphal procession; and
    straightway   965
Father Felician advanced with Evangeline, greeting
    the old man
Kindly and oft, and recalling the past, while Basil,
    enraptured,

Hailed with hilarious joy his old companions and gos-
    sips,
Laughing loud and long, and embracing mothers and
    daughters.
Much they marvelled to see the wealth of the ci-devant
    blacksmith,   97
All his domains and his herds, and his patriarchal
    demeanor;
Much they marvelled to hear his tales of the soil and
    the climate,
And of the prairies, whose numberless herds were his
    who would take them;
Each one thought in his heart, that he, too, would go
    and do likewise.
Thus they ascended the steps, and, crossing the breezy
    veranda,   975
Entered the hall of the house, where already the sup-
    per of Basil
Waited his late return; and they rested and feasted
    together.

  Over the joyous feast the sudden darkness de-
    scended.
All was silent without, and, illuming the landscape
    with silver,
Fair rose the dewy moon and the myriad stars; but
    within doors,   98
Brighter than these, shone the faces of friends in the
    glimmering lamplight.
Then from his station aloft, at the head of the table,
.   the herdsman
Poured forth his heart and his wine together in endless
    profusion.
Lighting his pipe, that was filled with sweet Natchi-
    toches tobacco.

Thus he spake to his guests, who listened, and smiled
    as they listened : —   ₉₃₅
" Welcome once more, my friends, who long have been
    friendless and homeless,
Welcome once more to a home, that is better per-
    chance than the old one !
Here no hungry winter congeals our blood like the
    rivers;
Here no stony ground provokes the wrath of the
    farmer;
Smoothly the ploughshare runs through the soil, as a
    keel through the water.   ₉₉₀
All the year round the orange-groves are in blossom;
    and grass grows
More in a single night than a whole Canadian summer.
Here, too, numberless herds run wild and unclaimed
    in the prairies;
Here, too, lands may be had for the asking, and
    forests of timber
With a few blows of the axe are hewn and framed
    into houses.   ₉₉₅
After your houses are built, and your fields are yellow
    with harvests,
No King George of England shall drive you away from
    your homesteads,
Burning your dwellings and barns, and stealing your
    farms and your cattle."
Speaking these words, he blew a wrathful cloud from
    his nostrils,
While his huge, brown hand came thundering down
    on the table,   ₁₀₀₀
So that the guests all started ; and Father Felician,
    astounded,
Suddenly paused, with a pinch of snuff half-way to
    his nostrils.

But the brave Basil resumed, and his words were
    milder and gayer : —
"Only beware of the fever, my friends, beware of the
    fever!
For it is not like that of our cold Acadian climate,   100c
Cured by wearing a spider hung round one's neck in r
    nutshell!"
Then there were voices heard at the door, and foot
    steps approaching
Sounded upon the stairs and the floor of the breezy
    veranda.
It was the neighboring Creoles and small Acadian
    planters,
Who had been summoned all to the house of Basil the
    herdsman.   1010
Merry the meeting was of ancient comrades and
    neighbors :
Friend clasped friend in his arms; and they who
    before were as strangers,
Meeting in exile, became straightway as friends to each
    other,
Drawn by the gentle bond of a common country
    together.
But in the neighboring hall a strain of music, pro-
    ceeding   1015
From the accordant strings of Michael's melodious
    fiddle,
Broke up all further speech. Away, like children
    delighted,
All things forgotten beside, they gave themselves to
    the maddening
Whirl of the dizzy dance, as it swept and swayed to
    the music,
Dreamlike, with beaming eyes and the rush of flutter-
    ing garments.   1020

Meanwhile, apart, at the head of the hall, the priest
    and the herdsman
Sat, conversing together of past and present and
    future ;
While Evangeline stood like one entranced, for within
    her
Olden memories rose, and loud in the midst of the
    music
Heard she the sound of the sea, and an irrepres-
    sible sadness   1025
Came o'er her heart, and unseen she stole forth into
    the garden.
Beautiful was the night. Behind the black wall of
    the forest,
Tipping its summit with silver, arose the moon. On
    the river
Fell here and there through the branches a tremulous
    gleam of the moonlight,
Like the sweet thoughts of love on a darkened and
    devious spirit.   1030
Nearer and round about her, the manifold flowers
    of the garden
Poured out their souls in odors, that were their prayers
    and confessions
Unto the night, as it went its way, like a silent
    Carthusian.

1033. The Carthusians are a monastic order founded in the
twelfth century, perhaps the most severe in its rules of all religious societies. Almost perpetual silence is one of the vows; the
monks can talk together but once a week ; the labor required of
them is unremitting and the discipline exceedingly rigid. The
first monastery was established at Chartreux near Grenoble in
France, and the Latinized form of the name has given us the
word Carthusian.

Fuller of fragrance than they, and as heavy with
    shadows and night-dews,
Hung the heart of the maiden. The calm and the
    magical moonlight   1035
Seemed to inundate her soul with indefinable long-
    ings,
As, through the garden gate, and beneath the shade
    of the oak-trees,
Passed she along the path to the edge of the measure-
    less prairie.
Silent it lay, with a silvery haze upon it, and fire-flies
Gleamed and floated away in mingled and infinite
    numbers.   1040
Over her head the stars, the thoughts of God in the
    heavens,
Shone on the eyes of man, who had ceased to marvel
    and worship,
Save when a blazing comet was seen on the walls of
    that temple,
As if a hand had appeared and written upon them,
    " Upharsin."
And the soul of the maiden, between the stars and
    the fire-flies,   1045
Wandered alone, and she cried, "O Gabriel! O my
    beloved !
Art thou so near unto me, and yet I cannot behold
    thee ?
Art thou so near unto me, and yet thy voice does not
    reach me ?
Ah! how often thy feet have trod this path to the
    prairie !
Ah! how often thine eyes have looked on the wood-
    lands around me !   1050
Ah! how often beneath this oak, returning from labor,

Thou hast lain down to rest, and to dream of me in
    thy slumbers!
When shall these eyes behold, these arms be folded
    about thee?"
Loud and sudden and near the notes of a whippoor-
    will sounded
Like a flute in the woods; and anon, through the
    neighboring thickets,   1055
Farther and farther away it floated and dropped into
    silence.
" Patience!" whispered the oaks from oracular cav-
    erns of darkness;
And, from the moonlit meadow, a sigh responded,
    " To-morrow!"

    Bright rose the sun next day; and all the flowers
    of the garden
Bathed his shining feet with their tears, and anointed
    his tresses   1060
With the delicious balm that they bore in their vases
    of crystal.
"Farewell!" said the priest, as he stood at the
    shadowy threshold;
"See that you bring us the Prodigal Son from his
    fasting and famine,
And, too, the Foolish Virgin, who slept when the
    bridegroom was coming."
'Farewell!" answered the maiden, and, smiling, with
    Basil descended   1065
Down to the river's brink, where the boatmen already
    were waiting.
Thus beginning their journey with morning, and sun-
    shine, and gladness,
Swiftly they followed the flight of him who was speed-
    ing before them.

Blown by the blast of fate like a dead leaf over the
    desert.
Not that day, nor the next, nor yet the day that suc-
    ceeded,   1070
Found they trace of his course, in lake or forest or
    river,
Nor, after many days, had they found him ; but vague
    and uncertain
Rumors alone were their guides through a wild and
    desolate country ;
Till, at the little inn of the Spanish town of Adayes,
Weary and worn, they alighted, and learned from the
    garrulous landlord   1075
That on the day before, with horses and guides and
    companions,
Gabriel left the village, and took the road of the
    prairies.

IV.

Far in the West there lies a desert land, where the
    mountains
Lift, through perpetual snows, their lofty and lumi-
    nous summits.
Down from their jagged, deep ravines, where the
    gorge, like a gateway,   1080
Opens a passage rude to the wheels of the emigrant's
    wagon,
Westward the Oregon flows and the Walleway and
    Owyhee.
Eastward, with devious course, among the Wind-river
    Mountains,
Through the Sweet-water Valley precipitate leaps the
    Nebraska ;
And to the south, from Fontaine-qui-bout and the
    Spanish sierras,   1085

Fretted with sands and rocks, and swept by the wind
    of the desert,
Numberless torrents, with ceaseless sound, descend to
    the ocean,
Like the great chords of a harp, in loud and solemn
    vibrations.
Spreading between these streams are the wondrous
    beautiful prairies,
Billowy bays of grass ever rolling in shadow and sun-
    shine, 1090
Bright with luxuriant clusters of roses and purple
    amorphas.
Over them wandered the buffalo herds, and the elk
    and the roebuck ;
Over them wandered the wolves, and herds of rider-
    less horses ;
Fires that blast and blight, and winds that are weary
    with travel ;
Over them wander the scattered tribes of Ishmael's
    children, 1095
Staining the desert with blood ; and above their terri-
    ble war-trails
Circles and sails aloft, on pinions majestic, the vul-
    ture,
Like the implacable soul of a chieftain slaughtered
    in battle,
By invisible stairs ascending and scaling the heav-
    ens.
Here and there rise smokes from the camps of these
    savage maranders ; 1100
Here and there rise groves from the margins of swift-
    running rivers;
And the grim, taciturn bear, the anchorite monk of
    the desert,

Climbs down their dark ravines to dig for roots by
    the brook-side,
And over all is the sky, the clear and crystalline
    heaven,
Like the protecting hand of God inverted above
    them.   110.

Into this wonderful land, at the base of the Ozark
    Mountains,
Gabriel far had entered, with hunters and trappers
    behind him.
Day after day, with their Indian guides, the maiden
    and Basil
Followed his flying steps, and thought each day to
    o'ertake him.
Sometimes they saw, or thought they saw, the smoke
    of his camp-fire   1110
Rise in the morning air from the distant plain; but
    at nightfall,
When they had reached the place, they found only
    embers and ashes.
And, though their hearts were sad at times and their
    bodies were weary,
Hope still guided them on, as the magic Fata Morgana
Showed them her lakes of light, that retreated and
    vanished before them.   1115

1114. The Italian name for a meteoric phenomenon nearly
allied to a mirage, witnessed in the Straits of Messina, and less
frequently elsewhere, and consisting in the appearance in the
air over the sea of the objects which are upon the neighboring
coasts. In the southwest of our own country, the mirage is very
common, of lakes which stretch before the tired traveller, and
the deception is so great that parties have sometimes beckoned
to other travellers, who seemed to be wading knee-deep, to come
over to them where dry land was

Once, as they sat by their evening fire, there silently
entered
Into the little camp an Indian woman, whose features
Wore deep traces of sorrow, and patience as great as
her sorrow.
She was a Shawnee woman returning home to her
people,
From the far-off hunting-grounds of the cruel Ca-
manches, 1120
Where her Canadian husband, a coureur-des-bois,
had been murdered.
Touched were their hearts at her story, and warmest
and friendliest welcome
Gave they, with words of cheer, and she sat and
feasted among them
On the buffalo-meat and the venison cooked on the
embers.
But when their meal was done, and Basil and all his
companions, 1125
Worn with the long day's march and the chase of the
deer and the bison,
Stretched themselves on the ground, and slept where
the quivering fire-light
Flashed on their swarthy cheeks, and their forms
wrapped up in their blankets,
Then at the door of Evangeline's tent she sat and repeated
Slowly, with soft, low voice, and the charm of her Indian accent, 1130
All the tale of her love, with its pleasures, and pains,
and reverses.
Much Evangeline wept at the tale, and to know that
another
Hapless heart like her own had loved and had been
disappointed.

Moved to the depths of her soul by pity and woman's
    compassion,
Yet in her sorrow pleased that one who had suffered
    was near her,   1135
She in turn related her love and all its disasters.
Mute with wonder the Shawnee sat, and when she had
    ended
Still was mute; but at length, as if a mysterious hor
    ror
Passed through her brain, she spake, and repeated the
    tale of the Mowis;
Mowis, the bridegroom of snow, who won and wedded
    a maiden,   1140
But, when the morning came, arose and passed from
    the wigwam,
Fading and melting away and dissolving into the sun-
    shine,
Till she beheld him no more, though she followed far
    into the forest.
Then, in those sweet, low tones, that seemed like a
    weird incantation,
Told she the tale of the fair Lilinau, who was wooed
    by a phantom,   1145
That, through the pines o'er her father's lodge, in the
    hush of the twilight,
Breathed like the evening wind, and whispered love to
    the maiden,
Till she followed his green and waving plume through
    the forest,
And nevermore returned, nor was seen again by her
    people.

1145. The story of Lilinau and other Indian legends will be
found in H. R. Schoolcraft's *Algic Researches.*

Silent with wonder and strange surprise, Evangeline
    listened   1150
To the soft flow of her magical words, till the region
    around her
Seemed like enchanted ground, and her swarthy guest
    the enchantress.
Slowly over the tops of the Ozark Mountains the
    moon rose,
Lighting the little tent, and with a mysterious splen-
    dor
Touching the sombre leaves, and embracing and filling
    the woodland.   1155
With a delicious sound the brook rushed by, and the
    branches
Swayed and sighed overhead in scarcely audible whis-
    pers.
Filled with the thoughts of love was Evangeline's
    heart, but a secret,
Subtile sense crept in of pain and indefinite terror,
As the cold, poisonous snake creeps into the nest of
    the swallow.   1160
It was no earthly fear. A breath from the region of
    spirits
Seemed to float in the air of night; and she felt for a
    moment
That, like the Indian maid, she, too, was pursuing a
    phantom.
With this thought she slept, and the fear and the
    phantom had vanished.

    Early upon the morrow the march was resumed, and
    the Shawnee   1165
Said, as they journeyed along, — "On the western
    slope of these mountains

Dwells in his little village the Black Robe chief of
    the Mission.
Much he teaches the people, and tells them of Mary
    and Jesus ;
Loud laugh their hearts with joy, and weep with pain
    as they hear him."
Then, with a sudden and secret emotion, Evangeline
    answered,   1170
" Let us go to the Mission, for there good tidings
    await us ! "
Thither they turned their steeds ; and behind a spur
    of the mountains,
Just as the sun went down, they heard a murmur of
    voices,
And in a meadow green and broad, by the bank of a
    river,
Saw the tents of the Christians, the tents of the Jesuit
    Mission.   1175
Under a towering oak, that stood in the midst of the
    village,
Knelt the Black Robe chief with his children. A
    crucifix fastened
High on the trunk of the tree, and overshadowed by
    grapevines,
Looked with its agonized face on the multitude kneel-
    ing beneath it.
This was their rural chapel.   Aloft, through the intri-
    cate arches   1180
Of its aerial roof, arose the chant of their vespers,
Mingling its notes with the soft susurrus and sighs of
    the branches.
Silent, with heads uncovered, the travellers, nearer
    approaching,
Knelt on the swarded floor, and joined in the evening
    devotions.

But when the service was done, and the benediction
    had fallen 1185

Forth from the hands of the priest, like seed from the
    hands of the sower,

Slowly the reverend man advanced to the strangers
    and bade them

Welcome; and when they replied, he smiled with be-
    nignant expression,

Hearing the homelike sounds of his mother-tongue in
    the forest,

And, with words of kindness, conducted them into his
    wigwam. 1190

There upon mats and skins they reposed, and on cakes
    of the maize-ear

Feasted, and slaked their thirst from the water-gourd
    of the teacher.

Soon was their story told; and the priest with solem-
    nity answered : —

" Not six suns have risen and set since Gabriel, seated

On this mat by my side, where now the maiden re-
    poses, 1195

Told me this same sad tale ; then arose and continued
    his journey ! "

Soft was the voice of the priest, and he spake with an
    accent of kindness ;

But on Evangeline's heart fell his words as in winter
    the snow-flakes

Fall into some lone nest from which the birds have
    departed.

" Far to the north he has gone," continued the priest ;
    " but in autumn, 1200

When the chase is done, will return again to the Mis-
    sion."

Then Evangeline said, and her voice was meek and
    submissive,

" Let me remain with thee, for my soul is sad and af-
    flicted."
So seemed it wise and well unto all; and betimes on
    the morrow,
Mounting his Mexican steed, with his Indian guides
    and companions,   1205
Homeward Basil returned, and Evangeline stayed at
    the Mission.

  Slowly, slowly, slowly the days succeeded each
    other, —
Days and weeks and months; and the fields of maize
    that were springing
Green from the ground when a stranger she came,
    now waving about her,
Lifted their slender shafts, with leaves interlacing,
    and forming   1210
Cloisters for mendicant crows and granaries pillaged
    by squirrels.
Then in the golden weather the maize was husked,
    and the maidens
Blushed at each blood-red ear, for that betokened a
    lover,
But at the crooked laughed, and called it a thief in
    the corn-field.
Even the blood-red ear to Evangeline brought not her
    lover.   1215
' Patience!" the priest would say; " have faith, and
    thy prayer will be answered!
Look at this vigorous plant that lifts its head from
    the meadow,
See how its leaves are turned to the north, as true as
    the magnet;

This is the compass-flower, that the finger of God has
  planted
Here in the houseless wild, to direct the traveller's
  journey   122⁶
Over the sea-like, pathless, limitless waste of the
  desert.
Such in the soul of man is faith.   The blossoms of
  passion,
Gay and luxuriant flowers, are brighter and fuller of
  fragrance,
But they beguile us, and lead us astray, and their
  odor is deadly.
Only this humble plant can guide us here, and here-
  after   1225
Crown us with asphodel flowers, that are wet with the
  dews of nepenthe."

So came the autumn, and passed, and the winter —
  yet Gabriel came not ;
Blossomed the opening spring, and the notes of the
  robin and bluebird
Sounded sweet upon wold and in wood, yet Gabriel
  came not.
But on the breath of the summer winds a rumor was
  wafted   123⁰

1219. *Silphium laciniatum* or compass-plant is found on the
prairies of Michigan and Wisconsin and to the south and west,
and is said to present the edges of the lower leaves due north
and south.

1226. In early Greek poetry the asphodel meadows were
haunted by the shades of heroes. See Homer's *Odyssey,* xxiv.
13, where Pope translates : —

" In ever flowering meads of Asphodel."

The asphodel is of the lily family, and is known also by the
name king's spear.

Sweeter than song of bird, or hue or odor of blos-
    som.

Far to the north and east, it said, in the Michigan
    forests,

Gabriel had his lodge by the banks of the Saginaw
    River.

And, with returning guides, that sought the lakes of
    St. Lawrence,

Saying a sad farewell, Evangeline went from the Mis-
    sion.   1235

When over weary ways, by long and perilous
    marches,

She had attained at length the depths of the Michigan
    forests,

Found she the hunter's lodge deserted and fallen to
    ruin !

    Thus did the long sad years glide on, and in sea-
    sons and places

Divers and distant far was seen the wandering
    maiden ; —   1240

Now in the Tents of Grace of the meek Moravian
    Missions,

Now in the noisy camps and the battle-fields of the
    army,

Now in secluded hamlets, in towns and populous
    cities.

Like a phantom she came, and passed away unremem-
    bered.

Fair was she and young, when in hope began the long
    journey ;   1245

Faded was she and old, when in disappointment it
    ended.

    1241. A rendering of the Moravian Gnadenhütten.

Each succeeding year stole something away from her
 beauty,
Leaving behind it, broader and deeper, the gloom and
 the shadow.
Then there appeared and spread faint streaks of gray
 o'er her forehead,
Dawn of another life, that broke o'er her earthly horizon,   1250
As in the eastern sky the first faint streaks of the
 morning.

v.

In that delightful land which is washed by the Delaware's waters,
Guarding in sylvan shades the name of Penn the
 apostle,
Stands on the banks of its beautiful stream the city
 he founded.
There all the air is balm, and the peach is the emblem
 of beauty,   1255
And the streets still reëcho the names of the trees of
 the forest,
As if they fain would appease the Dryads whose
 haunts they molested.
There from the troubled sea had Evangeline landed,
 an exile,
Finding among the children of Penn a home and a
 country.
There old René Leblanc had died; and when he
 departed,   1260
Saw at his side only one of all his hundred descendants.

1256. The streets of Philadelphia, as is well known, are many
of them, especially those running east and west, named for trees,
as Chestnut, Walnut, Locust, Spruce, Pine, etc.

Something at least there was in the friendly streets of
 the city,
Something that spake to her heart, and made her no
 longer a stranger ;
And her ear was pleased with the Thee and Thou of
 the Quakers,
For it recalled the past, the old Acadian country, 1265
Where all men were equal, and all were brothers and
 sisters.
So, when the fruitless search, the disappointed en
 deavor,
Ended, to recommence no more upon earth, uncom-
 plaining,
Thither, as leaves to the light, were turned her
 thoughts and her footsteps.
As from the mountain's top the rainy mists of the
 morning 1270
Roll away, and afar we behold the landscape below us,
Sun-illumined, with shining rivers and cities and ham-
 lets,
So fell the mists from her mind, and she saw the
 world far below her,
Dark no longer, but all illumined with love ; and the
 pathway
Which she had climbed so far, lying smooth and fair
 in the distance. 1275
Gabriel was not forgotten. Within her heart was his
 image,
Clothed in the beauty of love and youth, as last she
 beheld him,
Only more beautiful made by his deathlike silence and
 absence.
Into her thoughts of him time entered not, for it was
 not.

Over him years had no power; he was not changed,
    but transfigured;   1280
He had become to her heart as one who is dead, and
    not absent;
Patience and abnegation of self, and devotion to others,
This was the lesson a life of trial and sorrow had
    taught her.
So was her love diffused, but, like to some odorous
    spices,
Suffered no waste nor loss, though filling the air with
    aroma.   1285
Other hope had she none, nor wish in life, but to
Meekly follow, with reverent steps, the sacred feet of
    her Saviour.
Thus many years she lived as a Sister of Mercy; fre-
    quenting
Lonely and wretched roofs in the crowded lanes of
    the city,
Where distress and 'vant concealed themselves from
    the sunlight,   1290
Where disease and sorrow in garrets languished neg-
    lected.
Night after night when the world was asleep, as the
    watchman repeated
Loud, through the dusty streets, that all was well in
    the city,
High at some lonely window he saw the light of her
    taper.
Day after day, in the gray of the dawn, as slow
    through the suburbs   1295
Plodded the German farmer, with flowers and fruits
    for the market,
Met he that meek, pale face, returning home from its
    watchings.

Then it came to pass that a pestilence fell on the
    city,
Presaged by wondrous signs, and mostly by flocks of
    wild pigeons,
Darkening the sun in their flight, with naught in their
    craws but an acorn.   1300
And, as the tides of the sea arise in the month of Sep-
    tember,
Flooding some silver stream, till it spreads to a lake
    in the meadow,
So death flooded life, and, o'erflowing its natural mar-
    gin,
Spread to a brackish lake the silver stream of ex-
    istence.
Wealth had no power to bribe, nor beauty to charm,
    the oppressor ;   1305
But all perished alike beneath the scourge of his
    anger ; —
Only, alas ! the poor, who had neither friends nor at-
    tendants,
Crept away to die in the almshouse, home of the
    homeless.
Then in the suburbs it stood, in the midst of meadows
    and woodlands ; —

1298. The year 1793 was long remembered as the year when
yellow fever was a terrible pestilence in Philadelphia. Charles
Brockden Brown made his novel of *Arthur Mervyn* turn largely
upon the incidents of the plague, which drove Brown away from
home for a time.

1308. Philadelphians have identified the old Friends' almshouse on Walnut Street, now no longer standing, as that in which
Evangeline ministered to Gabriel, and so real was the story that
some even ventured to point out the graves of the two lovers.
See Westcott's *The Historic Mansions of Philadelphia*, pp. 101,
102.

Now the city surrounds it; but still, with its gateway
    and wicket   1310
Meek, in the midst of splendor, its humble walls seem
    to echo
Softly the words of the Lord : — "The poor ye al-
    ways have with you."
Thither, by night and by day, came the Sister of
    Mercy. The dying
Looked up into her face, and thought, indeed, to be-
    hold there
Gleams of celestial light encircle her forehead with
    splendor,   1315
Such as the artist paints o'er the brows of saints and
    apostles,
Or such as hangs by night o'er a city seen at a distance.
Unto their eyes it seemed the lamps of the city celes-
    tial,
Into whose shining gates erelong their spirits would
    enter.

    Thus, on a Sabbath morn, through the streets, de-
    serted and silent,   1320
Wending her quiet way, she entered the door of the
    almshouse.
Sweet on the summer air was the odor of flowers in
    the garden,
And she paused on her way to gather the fairest
    among them,
That the dying once more might rejoice in their fra-
    grance and beauty.
Then, as she mounted the stairs to the corridors,
    cooled by the east-wind,   1325
Distant and soft on her ear fell the chimes from the
    belfry of Christ Church,

While, intermingled with these, across the meadows
    were wafted

Sounds of psalms, that were sung by the Swedes in
    their church at Wicaco.

Soft as descending wings fell the calm of the hour on
    her spirit;

Something within her said, " At length thy trials are
    ended ; "   1330

And, with light in her looks, she entered the cham-
    bers of sickness.

Noiselessly moved about the assiduous, careful attend-
    ants,

Moistening the feverish lip, and the aching brow, and
    in silence

Closing the sightless eyes of the dead, and concealing
    their faces,

Where on their pallets they lay, like drifts of snow
    by the roadside.   1335

Many a languid head, upraised as Evangeline entered,

Turned on its pillow of pain to gaze while she passed,
    for her presence

Fell on their hearts like a ray of the sun on the walls
    of a prison.

And, as she looked around, she saw how Death, the
    consoler,

Laying his hand upon many a heart, had healed it
    forever.   1340

1328. The Swedes' church at Wicaco is still standing, the
oldest in the city of Philadelphia, having been begun in 1698.
Wicaco is within the city, on the banks of the Delaware River.
An interesting account of the old church and its historic associations will be found in Westcott's book just mentioned, pp. 56–67.
Wilson the ornithologist lies buried in the churchyard adjoining
the church.

Many familiar forms had disappeared in the night
time ;
Vacant their places were, or filled already by strangers.

Suddenly, as if arrested by fear or a feeling of
wonder,
Still she stood, with her colorless lips apart, while a
shudder
Ran through her frame, and, forgotten, the flowerets
dropped from her fingers, 1345
And from her eyes and cheeks the light and bloom of
the morning.
Then there escaped from her lips a cry of such terrible anguish,
That the dying heard it, and started up from their
pillows.
On the pallet before her was stretched the form of an
old man.
Long, and thin, and gray were the locks that shaded
his temples ; 1350
But, as he lay in the morning light, his face for a
moment
Seemed to assume once more the forms of its earlier
manhood ;
So are wont to be changed the faces of those who are
dying.
Hot and red on his lips still burned the flush of the
fever,
As if life, like the Hebrew, with blood had besprinkled
its portals, 1355
That the Angel of Death might see the sign, and pass
over.
Motionless, senseless, dying, he lay, and his spirit
exhausted

Seemed to be sinking down through infinite depths in
  the darkness,
Darkness of slumber and death, forever sinking and
  sinking.
Then through those realms of shade, in multiplied
  reverberations,   1360
Heard he that cry of pain, and through the hush that
  succeeded
Whispered a gentle voice, in accents tender and saint-
  like,
"Gabriel! O my beloved!" and died away into silence.
Then he beheld, in a dream, once more the home of
  his childhood;
Green Acadian meadows, with sylvan rivers among
  them,   1365
Village, and mountain, and woodlands; and, walking
  under their shadow,
As in the days of her youth, Evangeline rose in his
  vision.
Tears came into his eyes; and as slowly he lifted his
  eyelids,
Vanished the vision away, but Evangeline knelt by his
  bedside.
Vainly he strove to whisper her name, for the accents
  unuttered   1370
Died on his lips, and their motion revealed what his
  tongue would have spoken.
Vainly he strove to rise; and Evangeline, kneeling
  beside him,
Kissed his dying lips, and laid his head on her bosom.
Sweet was the light of his eyes; but it suddenly sank
  into darkness,
As when a lamp is blown out by a gust of wind at a
  casement.   1375

All was ended now, the hope, and the fear, and the
    sorrow,
All the aching of heart, the restless, unsatisfied
    longing,
All the dull, deep pain, and constant anguish of
    patience!
And, as she pressed once more the lifeless head to her
    bosom,
Meekly she bowed her own, and murmured, "Father,
    I thank thee!"   1380

Still stands the forest primeval; but far away from
    its shadow,
Side by side, in their nameless graves, the lovers are
    sleeping.
Under the humble walls of the little Catholic church-
    yard,
In the heart of the city, they lie, unknown and un-
    noticed.
Daily the tides of life go ebbing and flowing beside
    them,   1385
Thousands of throbbing hearts, where theirs are at
    rest and forever,
Thousands of aching brains, where theirs no longer
    are busy,
Thousands of toiling hands, where theirs have ceased
    from their labors,
Thousands of weary feet, where theirs have completed
    their journey!

Still stands the forest primeval; but under the
    shade of its branches   1390
Dwells another race, with other customs and language.

Only along the shore of the mournful and misty
      Atlantic
Linger a few Acadian peasants, whose fathers from
      exile
Wandered back to their native land to die in its
      bosom.
In the fisherman's cot the wheel and the loom are still
      busy;   1395
Maidens still wear their Norman caps and their kirtles
      of homespun,
And by the evening fire repeat Evangeline's story,
While from its rocky caverns the deep-voiced, neigh-
      boring ocean
Speaks, and in accents disconsolate answers the wail
      of the forest.

PRONOUNCING VOCABULARY

OF PROPER NAMES AND FOREIGN WORDS IN EVANGELINE.

The diacritical marks given below are those found in the latest edition of Webster's International Dictionary.

EXPLANATION OF MARKS.

A Dash (¯) above the vowel denotes the long sound.

A Curve (˘) above the vowel denotes the short sound.

A Circumflex Accent (ˆ) above the vowels a or u denotes the sound of a in câre or of u in tûrn ; above the vowel o it denotes the sound of o in ôrb.

A Dot (˙) above the vowel a denotes the sound of a in pȧst.

A Double Dot (¨) above the vowel a denotes the sound of a in stär.

A Double Dot (̤) below the vowel u denotes the sound of u in trụe.

A Wave (˜) above the vowel e denotes the sound of e in hẽr.

ṣ sounds like z.

ç sounds like s.

ġ sounds like j.

â, ê, ô are similar in sound to á, ē, ō, but are not pronounced so long.

Note that the pronunciation of French words can be given only approximately by means of signs and English equivalents. A living teacher is requisite to enable one to read and speak the language with elegance.

Abbé Guillaume Thomas Francis Raynal (Ăb-bā' gē-yōm', etc.).

Acadie (ä-kä-dē').

Ăccā'dĭȧ.

Ădā'yes.

Aelian (ē'lĭ-ăn).

Aix-la-Chapelle (āks-lä-shä-pĕl').

Amorphas (á-mȯr'fȧz).

Angelus Domini (ăn'jē-lŭs dŏm'ĭ-nĭ).

Ărcā'dĭa.

asphodel (ăs'fō-dĕl).

Atchafalaya (ăch-ȧ-fä-lī'ȧ).

Attakapas (ăt-tŭk'ȧ-paw).

Bacchantes (băk-kăn'tēz).

Bacchus (băk'ŭs).

Beau Séjour (bō sā-zhoor').

Bĕnĕdĭç'ĭtĕ.

Bĕn'edĭct Bĕllefŏntāine'.

Blŏm'ĭdŏn.

Briareus (brī'á-rūs).

Bruges (brụzh).

Cădiẑ'.

Cămăn'chĕg.

Cănărd'.

Cape Brĕt'ŏn.

Çĕl'tĭc.

Charente Inferieure (shär-änht' änh-fä-rē-ẽr').

Charnisay (shär-nĭ-zā').

Chartreux (shär-trẽ').

ci-devant (sē-dŭ-vänh′).
Cotĕlle′.
coureurs-des-bois (kōō′rēr-dā-bwä).
Contes Populaires (kônht pŏp-ṵ-lâr′).
couvre-feu (kōō′vr-fĕ).
Dante's Divina Commedia (dȳ - vē′ nä
    cŏm-mā′dĬ-ä).
Ducauroi (dṵ-kō-rwä′).
Evăn′gelïne.
Fä′tá Mörga′nä.
Father Felician (fĕ-lĬsh′Ĭ-ån).
Fontaine-qui-bout (fônh′tän-kĕ-bōō).
Gabriel Lajeunesse (lä-zhĕ-nĕs′).
Gaspereau (găs-pĕ-rō′).
Gayarré (gī-ä-rā′).
Gnadenhütten (gnä-dĕn-hṵt′ĕn).
Grand-Pré (gränh-prā′).
Hĕrŏd′ŏtŭs.
Horae Hellenicae (hō′rē hĕl-lĕn′Ĭ-sē).
Isaac de Razilli (dĕ rä-zē-yē′).
Kavanagh (kăv′á-nä).
La Clé du Caveau (lä klā dṵ kä-vō′).
La Gazza Ladra (lä găt′zä lä′drä).
Lä Häve.
Lä Sälle.
Le Carillon de Dunkerque (lĕ kär-ē-
    yônh′ dĕ dṵn-kĕrk′).
Létiche (lā-tēsh′).
Lilinau (lē′lĬ-nō).
Louisburg (lōō′Ĭ-bŭrg).
Loup-garou (lōō-gär-ōō′).
maître de chapelle (mā′tr dĕ shä-pĕl′).
Melita (mĕ-lē′ta).
Minas Basin (mē′năs basin).
Mowis (mō′wĕs).

Natchitoches (năck′ō-tŏsh).
nĕpēn′thē.
Opelousas (ŏp-ē-lōō′säs).
Outre-Mer (ōōtr-mâr′).
Owȳ′hee.
Păssămáquŏd′dy.
Pierre Capelle (pē-âr′ kä-pĕl′).
PĬs′ĬquĬd.
Plaquemine, Bayou of (plăk-mēn′, bi′ōō)
Pluquet (plṵ-kā′).
Pointe Coupée (pwănht kōō-pā′).
Poitou (pwä-tōō′).
René Leblanc (rē-nā′ lē-blänhk′).
Rochelle (rŏ-shĕll′).
Rossini (rŏs-sē′nē).
St. Maur (sänh mōr′).
Saintonge (sänh-tônhzh′).
Sām′sŏu Ăgônĭs′tēṣ.
seraglio (sē-răl′yŏ).
Siena (sē-ā′nä).
Silphium laciniatum (sĬl′fĬ-ŭm lä-sĬn-Ĭ-
    ā′tŭm).
Straits of Messina (mēs-sē′nä).
Têche (tāsh).
Tous les Bourgeois de Chartres (tōō lä
    bōōr-zhwä′ dĕ shärtr).
Upharsin (ū-fär′sĬn).
Utrecht (ū′trĕkt).
Vendée (vänh-dā′).
voyageur (vwä-yä-zhĕr′).
Wachita (wŏsh′ĕ-taw).
Walleway (wŏll′ĕ-wä).
wĕre-wolf.
Wicaco (wē-kä′kŏ).
Xerxes (zĕrks′ēz).

The Riverside Literature Series.

[A list of the first fifty-eight numbers is given on the next page.]

Also, bound in linen : ** 25 cents. * 11 and 63 in one vol., 40 cents ; likewise 70 and 69, 55 and 67, 70 and 71, 89 and 90. ‡ Also in one vol., 40 cents. § Double Number, 40 cents ; linen, 50 cents. §§ Quadruple Number, 50 cents ; linen, 60 cents.

EXTRA NUMBERS.

The Riverside Literature Series.

With Introductions, Notes, Historical Sketches, and Biographical Sketches.
Each regular single number, paper, 15 cents.

Also, bound in linen : ** 25 cents. * 29 and 10 in one vol., 40 cents ; likewise 28 and 36, 4 and 5, 6 and 31, 15 and 30, 40 and 69, 57 and 58, 11 and 63. ‡ Also in one vol., 40 cents ; † ditto, 45 cents. ‡‡ 1, 4, and 30 also in one vol., 50 cents ; likewise 33, 34, and 35.

Continued on the inside of this cover.